THE WORST SPELLER IN JR. HIGH

CAROLINE JANOVER
Edited by Rosemary Wallner

Free Spirit PUBLISHING

Library of Congress Cataloging-in-Publication Data

Janover, Caroline.

    The worst speller in jr. high / by Caroline Janover ; edited by Rosemary Wallner.

    p.   cm.

    Summary: Starting out in the seventh grade, Katie Kelso finds herself trying to cope with her dyslexia and form a friendship with a very bright boy at school, while she and her family deal with her mother's cancer diagnosis.

    ISBN 0-915793-76-8

    [1. Dyslexia—Fiction. 2. Schools—Fiction. 3. Cancer—Fiction. 4. Friendship—Fiction. 5. Family life—Fiction.] I. Wallner, Rosemary, 1964–   ill. II. Title.

PZ7.J2445Wo 1995

[Fic]—dc20

94-26409

CIP

AC

Cover and book design by MacLean & Tuminelly

Editorial direction by Pamela Espeland

10 9 8 7 6 5 4 3 2

Printed in the United States of America

Free Spirit Publishing Inc.
400 First Avenue North, Suite 616
Minneapolis, MN 55401-1730
(612) 338-2068

*To my mother
Whose unfailing love and support
Inspire in me the courage
To persevere.*

1

Katie felt a spitball hit her in the neck. She narrowed her eyes, put both hands on her hips, and spun around to identify her attacker. Six smirking teenage boys sat in the back row of the classroom. Spud Larson tipped back in his desk chair and gave Katie a wink.

"Cut it out!" Katie whispered, thrilled to be hit by one of Spud's famous spitballs. Spud was by far the best-looking boy in the seventh grade. He wore Ralph Lauren polo shirts and had muscles like He-Man. Katie remembered when she and Spud had repeated first grade. Now Spud was one of the few boys in her class as tall as she was, even when she wore high heels. Katie considered Spud to be the leader of the P.K.'s, the popular kids. The P.K.'s went around tormenting the dorks. Katie had been a dork since elementary school.

"Knock it off!" Katie hissed.

"Poor Katie took a bull's-eye!" Spud grinned and ran his fingers through his sun-bleached hair. He ripped off a corner of his notebook paper and dampened the crinkled sheet with saliva. "Ready, boys?" he whispered, waiting for Miss Dalton to turn back to the blackboard. A spitball flew past Katie's desk and landed next to Miss Dalton's shoe.

Two days before, on the first day of school, Katie had made a pledge. She had promised herself that she would become a P.K. Not only that, she had vowed in her diary to begin dating boys by Thanksgiving, or by Christmas vacation at the latest.

Katie pretended to drop her pencil and picked up one of the spitballs from the floor. She put it in her pencil case. At lunch, she would show the spitball to her best friend, Corky. Corky would be impressed. The spitball would prove that Spud was already interested.

Miss Dalton, the homeroom teacher, rang a brass bell on her desk. Standing up, she straightened her suit skirt and said, "Please rise for the Pledge of Allegiance."

Katie glanced at her pinkies to find the broken fingernail. When she was three years old, her mother had squashed her right little finger in the car door by accident. Katie knew the mangled nail was on her right hand. She no longer confused "b" and "d" when she wrote words, because the "b" always went toward the hand with the crooked nail.

Katie raised her right hand and put it over her heart. When she got to the part about "one nation, under God," she felt something graze her shoulder and slip down the back of her summer sundress. A damp glob was on her back, right above her bra strap. Katie wiggled, and the spit-ball fell down past her half slip, out from under her dress, and onto the floor. Smothered giggles erupted from the back row.

Katie felt the heat rising up into her cheeks. She knew her face was turning bright red.

"With liberty, and justice for all," she continued and sat down quickly in her desk seat, as if nothing had happened.

Katie felt a wave of relief when the bell rang for first period. She stood up and slung her book bag over her shoulder. Nina was absent so she had no one to follow to English. Weaving her way into the traffic of teenagers in the hallway, Katie hurried down the corridor. Mr. Cherry had warned the students on the first day of school not to be late for class. Mr. Cherry had the reputation of being a hard grader and a strict teacher. Even though he wore a bow tie and tweed jacket, Katie thought he looked like a gangster because of his black beard and beady gerbil eyes.

Katie walked into the classroom and sat down at the desk nearest the door. A young teacher in a yellow dress with bows on it said, "*Bonjour, mademoiselle. Quelle classe voulez-vous?*"

Katie jumped up and backed hastily out the door. "I—I must be in the wrong classroom," she sputtered. She looked anxiously up and down the corridor. Only a few kids were left in the hallway.

"Excuse me," Katie said, stopping a tall kid with glasses. He looked like a ninth grader. "Can you tell me where to find Mr. Cherry's English class?"

"Oh, so you've got Mr. Pits for English. You poor kid. Well, to get to Pits' classroom, go up the north stairwell and take a right." The tall kid jogged off in the direction of the gym.

"Thanks!" called Katie. She walked to her right, then to her left.

"Excuse me." A girl chewing bubble gum walked quickly in Katie's direction. "Which way is north?"

The girl gave Katie a weird look, shrugged her shoulders, and kept on walking.

R-r-r-ring!

Katie felt her heart leap. The first-period warning bell echoed in her ear. She had one minute to find Mr. Cherry's class. A girl with frizzy hair, wearing high-heeled shoes, passed by holding her boyfriend's hand. "Where are the north stairs?" Katie asked desperately.

The girl pointed to the right. The boyfriend snickered as Katie ran down the corridor in the direction the girl had pointed.

"No running in the hallways, young lady!" a stern voice called from inside a classroom.

"Sorry, but I'm late. I'm lost. I can't find my English class."

"Who is your teacher?" A thin man with a mustache came to the door. He had a mole on his chin with a curly black hair growing out of it.

"Uh—my teacher's name is Mr. Pits. I mean, Mr. Cherry. Some girl just told me to go up the right stairs."

"You mean the left stairs."

"No, she said to go on the right stairs."

"Upperclassmen take delight in confounding younger classmen. Go left, young lady, go left."

Katie ran back to the left. "And stop running!" he added.

Perspiration dripped down Katie's neck and made two half-moon stains under the arms of her sundress. She wiped her forehead with the back of her hand and raced up the north stairs.

R-r-r-ring!

The last bell blasted in her ear. One by one, doors closed along the corridor as the teachers began their first-period classes. Alone in the hallway, Katie looked frantically in both directions. She wished she were back in elementary school, where she knew how to find every single classroom. Katie considered going to the nurse. She could sneeze and tell the nurse she was having one of her allergy attacks, or perhaps a migraine headache. She could go home and watch television instead of walking late into Mr. Cherry's English class.

Katie felt a hand on her shoulder. "Can I help you? You look a little confused." A black man with a briefcase smiled down at her.

"Well, I'm looking for my period one English class. Mr. Cherry is my teacher," she stammered, almost in tears.

"It's not easy to find your way around this building, especially the first week of school. I get the north and south stairwells confused myself, and I've been teaching at George Washington Junior High for twenty-six years."

Katie wished this man was her English teacher instead of Mr. Cherry. Cherry would probably send her to early-morning detention or mark her down a whole grade for tardiness. She might even have to go to the principal. In elementary school, she had never been tardy once.

"Mr. Cherry's classroom is at the end of the hall to the right," said the man.

"Thanks," said Katie, forcing a smile. She looked for her squashed nail and found her right hand. At the end of the hall, she turned right and hurried past the rotten-egg smell in the chemistry lab. Katie stood in front of Mr. Cherry's classroom door. She took a deep breath and knocked hesitantly.

2

Katie looked at her reflection in the window of Mr. Cherry's classroom door. Her waist-length, chestnut-red hair hung limply over her shoulders. Her sundress felt damp and wrinkled.

Katie knew she looked older than thirteen. Her cousin Simon said she looked just like the rock star who sang "Lovin' Ways" on the music cable channel. It was embarrassing to be seen by boys when she didn't feel her prettiest. Katie knocked again on the classroom door.

"Enter!" shouted Mr. Cherry in an impatient voice.

"I—I'm sorry I'm late, I got a little lost."

"Do I assume this will never happen again, Miss Kelso?"

"Oh, yes sir!" Katie looked at the floor and nodded her head vigorously. She sat down at the only empty desk, directly in front of Mr. Cherry.

Katie put the strap of her book bag over the chair and looked around the room. Spud was sitting in the back row tipping back in his chair. He ran his fingers through his wavy blond hair and winked at her. Tossing her hair over her shoulder, Katie hid a quick smile and turned her head to face the front of the classroom.

Mr. Cherry stood in front of his desk, looking just like an English teacher in college. Unbuttoning his tweed jacket, he took a pile of papers out of his briefcase.

"I corrected your first-day-of-the-year themes and I see we have our work cut out for us. Besides assigning four novels, three plays, poetry selections, and a biography, I plan to teach this class to write. We will hone work and study skills, and engender an appreciation for literature."

When Meghan, the girl next to her, whispered, "What does hone mean?" Katie just shrugged her shoulders. Sitting in the front row, she didn't dare answer. Meghan had been her friend since the fifth grade. She was part of the dorks—a real brain. If Meghan was confused by Mr. Cherry, Katie felt she had no hope.

"Please turn to page 18 in your English anthology and read the short story entitled *The Tell-Tale Heart*, by Edgar Allan Poe. I will give you fifteen minutes to read this story silently. I will then ask you to summarize the action and describe the style, symbolism, tension, and tone that Poe created in this story."

Katie took the thick English anthology out of her book bag. She opened the book to page 81 and began to read. After a page, she scratched her head. *This story is about lapdogs in Antarctica, not about a heart*, she thought to her-

8

self. Katie looked around the room and saw that most kids were on a page with an illustration of a man kneeling at a door with a lantern. Quickly she scanned the first pages of the book until she came to the illustration of the man. She turned back to page 18 and began reading the story from the beginning. Katie knew she'd never read seven pages of small print in fifteen minutes, especially now that she'd spent five minutes on lapdogs. In elementary school, the teachers understood about her learning difference. They gave her extra time for reading assignments. In junior high, the teachers didn't seem to care.

Katie felt a pencil poke her in the back. She turned around and saw Harvey Huddlestein. With his eyes, he pointed to a crumpled note on the floor. Katie glanced up. Mr. Cherry was writing words she couldn't sound out on the blackboard. Katie leaned down and casually picked up the note. She slipped it inside her anthology and read, "At 9:28 brop your pencils. Pass it no."

Katie looked up at the clock. It was 9:20. She folded the paper, checked to see that Mr. Cherry's back was turned, and tossed the note to Meghan. It landed in her lap. Meghan read the note and handed it to a boy biting his fingernails. Katie watched out of the corner of her eye as the note traveled up and down the rows. The story about the tell-tale heart was hard reading. Katie knew she had to go slowly and underline with a highlighter the important ideas and the main characters. Drawing a time line or pictures of the main events in a story often helped Katie remember the sequence of the plot. But if she took the time now to draw a time line or write a paragraph summary, she knew she would never get to page 24.

Katie imagined being called on. What if Spud found out she was a poor reader? She hadn't been in a class with him for years. After they both repeated first grade, he'd gone to a different elementary school, the one on the fancy side of town.

Mr. Cherry turned to the class. "You have four minutes to finish up your reading assignment," he announced loudly.

Katie was on page 21, three pages to go. It was 9:23. She glanced around the room. Most kids were on a page with an illustration of a man hammering down floor-boards. When Meghan closed her book, Katie closed her book, too. She put on a confident look and waited for the other students to finish their assignment.

Mr. Cherry buttoned his jacket and scratched his beard. "What is the emotional foreshadowing that the author used to create tension in this story?" No one answered. Mr. Cherry repeated the question. "Think about it, class. By what means did Edgar Allan Poe create emotional foreshadowing?"

A new boy in a black T-shirt with a lightning bolt going through a skeleton's head raised his hand. "Poe used powerful descriptive symbolism, like—"

Katie heard a pencil drop. Another bounced on the floor next to Mr. Cherry's feet. She glanced at the clock. It was one second before 9:28. Mr. Cherry looked annoyed. What if he gave them all early-morning detention? She'd already been tardy. What if Mr. Cherry called her parents and accused her of disrupting the class, and being late, and not understanding the assignment, all in one day?

She glanced at Spud. He was tipping back in his chair, grinning. He nodded toward her, whispering, "Go on." If she didn't drop her pencil, Spud would never throw a spitball at her again. She'd never make it into the P.K. crowd. She'd be forced to hang out with the dorks for the rest of her life in George Washington Junior High. Pencils were dropping all over the room.

Katie let her pencil roll into her lap.

"It seems that a sudden force of gravity has mysteriously pulled pencils to the floor," said Mr. Cherry calmly. He walked up and down the aisles, picking up pencils one by one off the floor. "Anyone wishing to have his or her pencil returned can see me after class. I am eternally grateful to this class for having replenished my dwindling pencil collection, particularly in September, when the pencils have clean, fresh erasers." Mr. Cherry put the pencils in his top desk drawer. Katie glanced at the pencil in her lap. She slipped it into the pocket of her sundress. She kept her eyes on Mr. Cherry, with her best look of attention.

Mr. Cherry coughed once and began his lecture again. Over and over the kid in the black T-shirt with the lightning bolt raised his hand to answer Cherry's impossible questions about foreshadowing. He looked so thin in his baggy blue jeans that Katie wondered if he'd eaten any breakfast. Once she had heard about a boy in the fifth grade who was so poor that he had come to school hungry every day. It made Katie feel even worse to realize that some skinny kid who wore sunglasses to class and needed a haircut knew all the answers and she didn't have a clue what Cherry was talking about. The boy looked like the type who'd spent his entire life playing video games in a dimly lit arcade, not reading books by famous authors.

After the discussion of *The Tell-Tale Heart*, Mr. Cherry handed back the corrected themes written in class the first day of school. He put each white-lined paper face down on the student's desk. Katie picked her theme up carefully, so Meghan and the person behind her couldn't see the grade. Being born with dyslexia wasn't fair. Even when she tried her hardest, her spelling was terrible. The names of people and places fell out of her brain like sand pouring through a sifter. Katie peeked at her paper. It was covered with bright red "SP" marks. She drew a sigh of relief. At least she had passed. At the top of the page, Mr. Cherry had written in his bold handwriting, "You write with creative flair."

"Move it or lose it, sweetie pie," Spud said, grinning as he walked past Katie's desk on his way to second period. Katie smelled his lemon cologne and saw up close the muscles in his tan arms. Meghan had told her that Spud's father worked at the country club. When Spud wasn't on the golf course being a caddie, Meghan had said, he could swim in the pool and work out in the weight room all summer for free. Katie packed up her book bag and followed Spud down the north stairwell to the second-period math class. Math class was a relief, after English. Katie did well in math as long as she didn't have to memorize too many facts at once.

Katie had lunch fourth period. Her friend Corky had already saved her a place to sit. Katie moved her tray along the cafeteria line, picking out fruit, salad, and crackers, so she could eat the calories in the chocolate pudding for dessert.

Katie carried her tray over to the table. Corky's tray was piled with brownies even though she was on a diet and the chocolate made her complexion even worse.

"So, how was your morning?" Corky asked, cramming a brownie into her mouth.

"Awful. English is a real drag. Mr. Cherry is the pits, pardon the pun."

"Well, he's no worse than Miss Shapin," said Corky, pushing her glasses up her nose. "Any cute boys in homeroom?"

"Spud someone, I forget his last name. I remember him from ages ago."

"No kidding. Is he cute?"

"He's adorable. The kids call him Spud the Stud, but his real name is Norman. I think he likes me."

"How do you know that? How can you tell if a boy likes you?" Corky stopped chewing and paid close attention.

"He threw a spitball at me," Katie said proudly. She unzipped her pencil case and dropped the spitball into Corky's lap. "He's a real hacker, this guy Spud. He made us all drop our pencils, and then the Pit took every one of them away except for mine, because I snuck it into the pocket of my sundress."

"Hmm. That sounds entertaining." Corky took aim at the garbage can with the spitball. "Any other cool kids?"

Katie unclipped a list of names from her notebook. "Nina's mom is the president of the Home and School this year. She made a list of all the kids in homeroom. Can you imagine naming your child Brain?" Katie asked.

"I've never head of anyone at G.W. named Brain. Let me see that."

"You don't know this kid because he's new this year. All he wears are punk rock T-shirts and blue jeans with ripped knees. And dark glasses every day. I can't believe that his name is Brain, especially since he's brilliant! In English, he was the only kid who could answer the Pit's questions."

"Let me see that!" Corky grabbed the class list out of Katie's hand. "His name isn't Brain. His name is Brian. It says Brian Straus, right here."

Katie shook her head. "I do that all the time," she moaned. "I mix up the letters so my eyes read different words. I thought record albums said 'All rights reversed' until my dad told me they said 'All rights reserved.'"

"Well, let's call him Brain anyway." When Corky laughed, her braces glistened. "That way, no one else will have the foggiest idea who we're talking about."

"Great idea. Look over there, to your left, I mean to your right," Katie whispered suddenly. "That's Spud, the one I was telling you about. Don't look now; he's staring right at us."

"He's staring at you, you mean. You've got the looks, not me. Boys only pay attention to me when they want to copy my homework."

"No one has ever asked to copy my homework. You should be proud that kids think you're so intelligent," said Katie reassuringly.

"My mom thinks that one day I'll be beautiful, too, after I lose twenty pounds and get my braces off."

"My mom says I can get my ears pierced in the eighth grade. I think that's dumb. If I hadn't repeated the first grade, I'd be in the eighth grade right now. Mom won't even let me cut my hair."

"But Katie, you have beautiful hair. I'd die to have hair like yours."

"You'd die, all right. It's like wearing a blanket on top of your head all summer. I want my hair like Mary Ruth's, short and perky."

"Mary Ruth is a drip."

"She's a drip with gorgeous hair. She's a P.K. Ever notice how the boys swarm around Mary Ruth's locker? Have you ever seen a boy next to my locker?"

"Yeah. Fred."

"Fred's a good kid, even if he does have bulging frog eyes. I feel sorry for him." Katie put her empty salad plate and chocolate pudding cup back on the tray. Hoisting her book bag over her shoulder, she watched Spud stride toward them.

"What's up, dude?" he asked.

"I'm not a dude," said Katie, smiling coyly.

"Tomorrow, in Pit's class, start to hum real soft, like about 9:15. Pass the word." Spud patted Katie affectionately on the top of the head. He was a bit taller than Katie. He smelled like the men's cologne counter at the department store.

"Hey, dude, what's up?" called Spud as he went from table to table, sipping people's drinks, telling jokes, and begging for cookies. Katie noticed that he put his arm around two girls before the bell rang for the end of the lunch period.

As Katie left the lunchroom, she saw the Asian student from her homeroom sitting alone at a table by the cafeteria door.

"Did you have a good lunch?" she asked as she passed by his table.

"Good lunch?" echoed the boy.

"Did you eat a good lunch?" Katie pretended to put food in her mouth. "Good?" she repeated.

16

"Good," said the boy with a shy smile. He stood up and backed away from Katie.

"Hey, Wee Wee, get over here," cried a short kid in cowboy boots.

"Don't call him Wee Wee," said Katie. "That's not his name. What's your name?" she asked.

"My name Ping Dong Wee."

"So we can call him Wee Wee Dung," Georgie Mazio, the short kid in the cowboy boots, cried excitedly. He laughed so hard he choked on his chocolate milk.

"Stop teasing this kid," announced Katie sternly. "His name is Ping. How would you like someone to call you the wrong name?"

"Katie has a crush on the Chink," Spud cried. Without clearing their trays, Georgie and Spud walked away from the table. "See you later, sweetie pie," called Spud as he strode out of the cafeteria.

Katie flipped her hair over her shoulder. "Good-bye, Ping," she said. "Have a good afternoon."

"Good-bye," said Ping. "Good afternoon and good night," he added.

Katie smiled and walked back over to Corky's table. Corky was eating another brownie and talking to Meghan and Susannah.

"Want to hang out in front of Burger King after school?" asked Corky.

"Not today," said Katie. "I go to my tutor on Thursdays, and then my mom might want me to baby-sit. I get stuck with my brat brothers more than you can imagine."

"Your brothers are adorable," said Corky.

"Sure they are. They're adorable when they're sound asleep."

"Call me the minute you get home."

"I'll call you after my tutor. I'm going to make her explain *The Tell-Tale Heart*. I've got to understand symbolism that only that new kid, Brain, can figure out."

As Katie walked out the cafeteria door, she saw Ping standing alone in the hall. He looked so small and confused it made her want to cry.

4

After meeting with her tutor, Katie pedaled her bike up her steep gravel driveway. She and her family had lived in the same house on Front Street ever since they moved to North Kent, Massachusetts, the year Katie finished kindergarten. Propping her bike against the garage door, Katie heard the telephone ringing in the kitchen. She grabbed her book bag and pushed open the back screen door.

"Hello?" Katie panted into the telephone receiver.

"Katie! Why didn't you call? I've been waiting for you to call for hours."

"But Corky, I just walked in the door! I stayed at my tutor's a bit longer so we could talk about the social studies report and *The Tell-Tale Heart*." Katie slung her heavy book bag up onto the kitchen table and plopped down on one of the chairs.

"I wish I had a tutor," said Corky.

"You don't need a tutor. You're a brain! You get straight A's, except in gym." Mozart, the family dog, climbed stiffly out of his basket and put his head on Katie's lap.

"I've got news," said Corky. "Remember that kid named Brian in your homeroom?"

"You mean Brain?"

"Exactly. Are you ready for this?"

"What? Tell me!" Mozart began to lick Katie on the ankle.

"He's loaded. He's so rich, he's got a chauffeur. He drives around in a stretch limo with a TV antenna on the back!"

"How do you know all this?" Katie asked excitedly.

"Because I saw it with my own eyes. Brian got into the limo about two blocks from G.W., where no one could see him."

"Oh, my God!" cried Katie. "I don't believe it! He looks like such a slob!"

"He kind of darted into the car," continued Corky. "I was walking Muffin. I saw the whole thing with my own eyes."

"I wonder where he lives?" Katie held the telephone under her chin, unzipped her L. L. Bean book bag, and took out the class list. "It says here his address is 22 Bella Vista Drive," she said. "Isn't that the winding road where we sat on the stone wall that day we went Rollerblading?"

"Yeah, that's the place," said Corky. "Remember you fell and got a bloody knee and almost didn't want to skate back? Well, that's the street Brian lives on."

"But that street has nothing but mansions on it."

"I told you, he's loaded. Only millionaires live on Bella Vista Drive."

Mrs. Kelso walked into the kitchen. "Kate, may I please use the telephone?" she asked.

"But Mom, this is important. I'm talking to Corky about Brain."

"Who?"

"Oh, you wouldn't understand. I'll be through in a minute." Katie turned her back to her mother. "We could ride our bikes up to Bella Vista," she whispered into the telephone.

Mrs. Kelso wiped the kitchen counter with her yellow sponge. Katie sensed she was annoyed. "Please, Kate, I've got to order more cane for my bassoon reeds before the music store closes at five."

Mrs. Kelso sponged out the sink, then sat down on a kitchen chair and unzipped the case that held her bassoon.

Katie turned around and watched as her mother fitted a new reed into the mouthpiece of the instrument. Her mother played second bassoon in the Boston Symphony Orchestra. She blew three notes. Mozart walked over and tried to push the bassoon away with his nose. Mrs. Kelso patted Mozart on the head and waited for the telephone.

"Corky, my mom needs the telephone. I'll call you later." Katie hung up the phone and clipped the class list back onto her binder.

"Kate, can you baby-sit Sam and Willy again tonight?" Mrs. Kelso asked. "Your father will be late, and I've got a seven o'clock rehearsal. I won't be home until after eleven."

"What time is Dad coming home?" Katie asked.

"He's got a dinner meeting in Boston. He won't be home until late."

"But who's going to help me with my homework? I've got to memorize twenty vocabulary words for English, and I've got to know *The Tell-Tale Heart* by heart!"

"Kate, you know Thursday nights are impossible. By the time you get home from the tutor, I've got to get supper on the table, and then rush out the door for Symphony Hall."

"But I thought Dad would help me."

"He's tied up in town. I'm sorry, sweetheart, but tonight you'll just have to manage on your own."

"You're never here when I need you!" cried Katie. "You know I have dyslexia, and I need you to drill me, and then you just take off and abandon me every time I desperately need your help."

"I could get up early and drill you before school," Mrs. Kelso suggested with a guilty look.

"Never mind. Just leave me with my two brat brothers and all the dishes, and hours and hours of homework!" Katie stood up, threw back her hair, and grabbed her book bag. She marched out of the kitchen. Mozart followed her, wagging his tail.

In her bedroom, Katie sat down at the desk and turned on the radio to the all-rock, all-the-time music station. She knew she'd have to memorize at least five vocabulary words before supper to have any chance of learning all twenty words by first period the next morning. She copied down the words on a piece of paper and said the definitions aloud. "Foreshadowing. Foreshadowing means hints inserted by the author to make the plot more credible. Irony. Irony means a striking contrast between apparent and real situations. Tone. Tone means the author's attitude toward what he is presenting."

Katie lifted Butterscotch, her gerbil, out of the cage and put her on the desk. She tested herself on the first five vocabulary words. She remembered that foreshadowing meant clues given by the author to make the plot more believable. Irony was a striking difference between something and something.

"Oh, I'll never get all these words right!" cried Katie, petting Butterscotch and putting her in her lap. "I'll just fail English, like I failed the first grade." She pictured being the only girl in her class forced to go to summer school. All the other kids would have baby-sitting jobs on the Cape, or travel with their families to Disney World, and she'd be sitting in a boiling hot classroom with the rest of the dorks.

"Time for supper!" Katie heard her mother's voice calling out the kitchen window to Sam and Willy.

Katie put Butterscotch back into her cage and walked down the stairs to the kitchen. "I'll never pass English!" she groaned as her mother put a plate of canned spaghetti in front of her.

"Kate, this is only the third day of school. Don't be so pessimistic. You've got your tutor, and extra support from Mrs. Chandler in the Learning Center. Besides that, you're a bright kid."

"How can you say I'm bright when I'm barely passing English?"

"I agree. How can you say she's bright?" said nine-year-old Sam as he sat down at the table. "Everybody knows that Katie is a dumb-dumb brain."

"Shut up!" Katie snapped at her younger brother.

"Mom, Katie told me to shut up!"

"Both of you, take a deep breath and enjoy your spaghetti," said Mrs. Kelso, pouring three glasses of milk. "Where is your little brother?"

"He's digging worms. He says he wants a pet," said Sam.

Willy pushed open the back screen door. His knees and hands were covered with mud. He was holding a fat, squirming worm in his hand. "Wook!" Willy cried proudly, holding the worm in his fist.

"Get a jar!" cried Sam. "We can make a worm habitat."

Mrs. Kelso took an empty plastic peanut butter jar from under the sink and handed it to Willy.

"Punch holes in the top of the jar," said Sam.

"So the worm can breathe," added Katie.

"Maybe the worm will think this is another worm, a rare white worm," said Sam, dropping a long piece of spaghetti from his plate into the jar.

Mrs. Kelso washed Willy's hands and lifted him into his high chair. Willy ripped off his bib and threw it on the floor. "Me big boy, no bib," he announced.

"Then put a dish towel under your chin," said his mother, "and eat your supper." Katie stood up and helped her little brother tie the dish towel around his neck.

Already spaghetti had gotten onto his lap. At two years old, Willy had red, curly hair and bright pink cheeks. Sam still had reddish-brown hair, but his curls had changed into long, thin strands that fell over his forehead and into his eyes. Now that he had started the fourth grade, Sam had begun to shower every morning and to part his wet hair on the right side with his dad's comb. By the time he got to school, however, the hair had fallen back into his eyes.

"You boys mind your sister. Kate is baby-sitting tonight."

"Oh, no, not her again," groaned Sam.

"This isn't my idea of heaven, either," said Katie. "Here, Mo! Come and get it!" She held out her plate with the rest of the spaghetti sauce. Mozart remained curled up in a ball in his basket by the refrigerator.

"Now we know he's totally deaf," said Sam. "If he won't come for food, it proves he can't hear anything."

"I wonder what made him go deaf?" Katie asked.

"Probably listening to Mom practice her bassoon all day," said Sam, stuffing another forkful of spaghetti into his mouth.

"Didn't the real Mozart go deaf?" asked Katie.

"No, that was Beethoven," replied her mother, glancing at the kitchen clock. "I've got to run," she said, picking up her bassoon case and pocketbook.

"Kiss, kiss!" Willy demanded, struggling to get out of his high chair.

"Don't let him loose," said Katie. "He'll get mud and spaghetti sauce all over the kitchen."

"I'd take him directly to the tub," suggested Mrs. Kelso as she kissed Willy on the top of his head. "Your dad will be late, too. Be sure to lock the doors after I leave." The door closed behind her.

Willy began to pound the tray of his high chair. "Mommy, Mommy!" he howled. "I want my mommy!" Tears rolled down his pink cheeks. As Katie reached to take him out of the high chair, he kicked her in the stomach with his muddy little feet. "I want my mommy!" he cried.

"Tough luck," said Katie, "I'm the boss now." Katie walked over and locked the kitchen door.

Sam looked annoyed. "You're not going to boss *me* around!"

"I'll make a deal. You can have 50 cents of my baby-sitting money if you either do the dishes or give Willy his bath. I've got more homework than a kid in college."

"I've got homework, too, you know," said Sam, stacking the dishes in the sink.

"My wum, I want my wum," cried Willy. Katie picked up the peanut butter jar and carried Willy and his pet worm upstairs to the bathtub. Filling the tub, she lifted her brother gently into the warm water.

"Tell me stowy," said Willy. He took a little wooden boat off the soap holder and began to run it through the waves. "Tell me stowy about twucks," he said. Katie rubbed Willy's face with a soapy washcloth. He squirmed, and then he shrieked and began to pound the water with his chubby fists.

"Okay, okay, I'll tell you a story," said Katie. Willy immediately sat still in the water. "Once upon a time there was a dump truck named Darby," Katie began. "It was red, with a lightning bolt painted on the side." Katie pretended that she was telling the story in front of TV cameras on "Sesame Street." She would be sitting in between Bert and Ernie and talking to a spellbound group of little kids. Katie loved to make up stories. Every night she wrote in her diary about her day. In her locked diary, she didn't have to worry about spelling words correctly or putting commas and capital letters in the right places. All she had to do was let her feelings and her imagination run loose.

"Telephone!" called Sam.

"Come watch Willy for a second," cried Katie. "Tell him about Darby the dump truck. This call could be important."

Sam came into the bathroom and knelt down beside the tub. "Let's make a hurricane," he said, swirling the bath water with his arms. Willy giggled.

When Katie returned, she saw the water sloshing over the side of the tub and spilling onto the bath mat.

"What on earth is going on here?" she cried. Katie pulled the plug and grabbed Willy out of the tub. "I talk to Nina for five minutes about homework and you guys make a complete mess!"

"Stop! Put the plug back in, quick!" yelled Sam.

"What for? His bath is over," said Katie, wrapping Willy in a towel.

"My wum! My wum!" sobbed Willy. "I want my wum."

Katie noticed the empty peanut butter jar sitting on top of the toilet seat cover. "Sam, did you put that poor innocent worm in the bathtub? You should be ashamed of yourself."

"I want my wum." Willy pushed away the towel and ran naked toward the back stairs.

"Stop him!" yelled Katie.

"I can't. He'll bite me."

"You'll have to get Willy another worm or we'll never get him to sleep," Katie scolded. She began to sop up the water on the bathroom floor with a sponge.

"I don't believe this!" muttered Sam as he hurried down the stairs. After about five minutes, he returned with a writhing brown worm. By now Katie had Willie safely in his crib. Sam ran to the bathroom for the empty peanut butter jar, dropped the worm into it, and handed it to Willy.

"You can sleep with the worm," Katie warned, "but only if you promise not to open the jar." She piled a stack of picture books in the corner of Willy's crib. He picked up a book about trucks and began to turn the pages.

"Me wead wum," he said happily.

Katie blew Willy a kiss and quietly shut the door.

CHAPTER

Katie flipped the switch on the blue desk lamp in her bedroom. She pulled the loose-leaf notebook out of her book bag and read over the assignments for each subject. In English, she had to reread *The Tell-Tale Heart* and study her vocabulary words. In social studies, she had to read pages 15 to 23 and write a paragraph about Pilgrims. In science, she had to draw prehistoric land formations.

She opened her social studies book. After reading the first chapter and underlining the main ideas with a yellow highlighter, she took out a white sheet of paper to write about the Pilgrims' first winter. Katie stared at the paper. No thoughts came into her head. When she had to write for school, her mind went dead. Thoughts only came into her brain when she told stories out loud or wrote in her diary. Katie sharpened her pencil and put Butterscotch on her lap. She stared at the white paper, her sharp pencil poised to write.

"I'll do my science assignment instead," she said out loud. Katie loved to draw. She began to sketch three types of land formations found in prehistoric times. Katie knew that the other kids thought she was the best artist in her class. They often begged Katie to draw her specialty, a galloping horse.

By 9:30, Katie could barely keep her eyes open. She lay her head on the blank sheet of paper for social studies and let her mind drift to Spud. She wondered what time he went to bed. How many girls had he kissed? She thought about when he had brushed past her in first-period English. Spud was the most awesome boy in the seventh grade. If she could get Spud to like her, she'd become a P.K. overnight. All the girls would envy her, even the girls with charge cards at Bloomingdale's.

Katie turned off her desk lamp. She washed up, checked on Willy, and climbed under her bedsheets. The September night, even in New England, was still too warm for a woolen blanket. Tomorrow she would wear her sundress with the elastic top, the one she could wear without a bra. Too sleepy to write in her diary, Katie turned off the lamp on her bedside table and pretended she was lying in Spud's suntanned arms.

"Wake up, Katie. Wake up!" Katie felt a hand violently shaking her arm.

"Leave me alone," she groaned.

"Get up quick! I hear a robber! I'm not kidding." Katie focused one open eye on Sam. He looked scared standing beside her in his blue Superman pajamas.

"It's your imagination." Katie pulled the sheets up over her head. "Go away. You interrupted an important dream."

"I heard a thud, and then I heard glass break. I'm getting Willy."

Katie sat up in bed and listened. She heard sounds at the bottom of the stairs. "Don't wake Willy up!" she whispered. "We'll never get him back to sleep."

"What should we do?" Sam asked.

Katie thought for a second. "Flush the toilet."

"I didn't pee!"

"You idiot, we'll flush the toilet to scare the robber. If he knows there are people in the house, he'll leave. Both cars are gone; he probably thinks the house is empty."

"How did he get in?"

"I locked all the doors," said Katie. "Did you lock the back door again after you got the worm for Willy?"

Sam shook his head.

"That's it! He saw all the lights out, and no cars in the driveway, and the back door wide open, so he just walked right in!"

"Do you think he's got a gun?"

Katie shook her head. "You flush the toilet," she whispered, "and I'll call the police." Katie tiptoed into her parents' bedroom and dialed the number beside the word "Police." She heard a man's voice answer.

"Come to 14 Front Street as fast as you can," Katie whispered urgently, her hands cupped over the mouthpiece of the telephone.

"You sound pretty desperate."

"Hurry. There's a robber in our living room!"

"Is he hungry, too?"

"How do I know if he's hungry? He's robbing our house!"

"What kind do you want?"

"Men with guns!" said Katie, forgetting to whisper.

"Look, lady, we usually don't deliver pizza with an armed driver."

"Isn't this the police station?" asked Katie.

"No, lady. This is Sal's Pizzeria in Lexington."

"I'm sorry. I'm—I'm calling the police," Katie stammered, hanging up the telephone. She looked at the number again. It said 555-3946. She remembered that she had dialed 555-3496. Katie picked up the phone and began to dial again.

"Wait, I hear a car," said Sam, tiptoeing into his parents' bedroom. "I think the police have arrived."

"Did you just hear a key?" asked Katie.

"How did the police get a key?" Sam asked, looking out the window.

"That's not the police. That's Dad's car. Dad's home! He could get killed by the robber! We've got to warn him!"

"I flushed the toilet," said Sam.

"Turn on the hall light. Dad will see the robber and hit him over the head with his briefcase."

Sam ran to the stair landing and flipped on the light. Their dad stood in the middle of the living room. He loosened his necktie and bent down to pick up a piece of broken glass. A broken vase and cut flowers from the garden were scattered all over the living room floor.

"Hey, kids! How did this happen?" he asked, looking up at Sam and Katie standing at the top of the stairs. "How come you two are still up? It's late."

"Dad! There was a robber!" cried Sam, racing down the stairs. He threw himself into his father's arms. Katie hurried down the stairs behind her brother. She looked around the room. Everything seemed in place. Nothing was missing, not even the television set or the precious silver tea service with her great-grandmother's initials on it.

"I bet Mozart walked into that antique end table," said Mr. Kelso, hugging his son. "I've noticed Mo has trouble seeing in the dark." He glanced at Mozart, who lay sound asleep on his favorite living room chair.

"He doesn't even hear us talking," said Sam, walking over to Mozart and patting him on the back.

Mozart woke up with a start. He wagged his tail and licked Sam in the face.

"We'd better clean up this mess before your mother gets home."

Katie went to the kitchen to get a roll of paper towel. When she returned, she leaned down to help her father pick up the broken glass and wilted petals. She noticed that the bald spot on the top of her Dad's head was getting even larger. "That table has always been a little rickety," she said, sopping up water from the rug.

"You kids go back to sleep. It's late. I'll finish up. I'll see you in the morning."

Katie hugged her dad. He smelled of cigar smoke from his business meeting. She walked back up the stairs to her bedroom. Her heart was still pounding hard underneath her summer nightgown.

Katie took her diary out from under the bed mattress. She tried the lock combination. She knew it by heart. Go right three turns and stop on six, go left one turn and stop on four, go right seven turns and stop at five. Katie opened her diary and began to write.

Setp. 10

Deer Dairy,

Today I went to sckool. It was hot and this boy named Spud threw a spit dall at me in homeroom. He's reel cool and I think he likes me. Corky told me this new kid named Brain is raelly rich. He has a showfur. Went to my tutor today and she says I need to work on stragedies to rember stupid words for Eng. I hate Eng esp. Mr. Pits. I don't think he likes me either. I'll make him LOVE me so I can pass Eng. It might take till T-giving to find Pits classroom. I got reely lost. Mom made me babysit again. She thinks Im her slave just becuz she plays in the orkestra and goes to rehersals almost every nite. I just want to be with my freinds and hang out with P.K.'s. I want to make new freinds and not just be with the dorks, only Corkie will still be my best freind becuz she has been sinse 1st gr. G.W. is reely hard. I wish I was back in Elem. sckool. I wish Spud would ask me out. He's reely cute only he teezes guys like Ping to get atenshon. Ever since I turned 13, I've wanted a boy freind. We thot we had a rober in the house only it was reely Motsart.

The End

Katie closed and locked her diary and shoved it back under the mattress. Climbing under her sheets, she turned out the light and quickly fell asleep.

CHAPTER

6

Sometime during the night, the rain had started. Katie borrowed her mother's umbrella and left for school early. She felt sure she had forgotten the combination to her new locker. It would take time to find a custodian to saw off the lock, and Katie did not want to be late for class. She threw her raincoat over her pink sundress with the elastic top. She had put her gym sneakers in her book bag so she could wear her summer sandals to school. This way people could see how her pink toenail polish perfectly matched the color of her dress. It didn't matter that her feet would get wet walking through the grass on the way to school.

Katie went directly to her locker. She wiggled her cold, damp toes and tried to repeat the locker combination. She turned the dial right to number 9, then left to number 25, and then right to 14. She yanked on the lock. Nothing happened. Katie looked up and down the corridor to see if people were watching. She had memorized "Sam, wedding, house" to help her remember the combination. Sam was 9, her mother got married when she was 25, and 14 was their house number on Front Street. Katie tried again. This time she turned the combination left to 9, right to 25, and left to 14. She pulled hard on the lock. To her relief, it snapped open. Katie put her gym shorts and sneakers into the locker and walked down the hall to homeroom.

"Good morning, Katie."

"Good morning, Miss Dalton," said Katie. She took the English vocabulary list out of her notebook and began to review the words she couldn't remember at breakfast time.

"How are you enjoying George Washington Junior High?" asked Miss Dalton, putting down her red pencil.

"It's okay, only I get lost sometimes in this building. It's pretty confusing in the beginning."

"Many seventh graders feel that way," Miss Dalton said reassuringly. Katie thought Miss Dalton looked pretty in her blue suit with the white ruffled blouse. She wondered why Miss Dalton had never married. Maybe she'd been a nun before she became a teacher. Maybe she'd lived in a convent and never been allowed to date until it was too late to find a man.

"Did you have a good summer?" asked Katie.

"Very enjoyable," said Miss Dalton. "I toured the British Isles. We spent a week in London and attended a good many Shakespearean plays."

"That's nice," said Katie. "My mom and dad took us to see a play once by Shakespeare in the Boston Common, called *Lots to Do About Something*."

"You mean *Much Ado About Nothing*."

"Yeah, that's it. I didn't understand it all, but I loved watching the people in the audience. We sat on a blanket and had a picnic. That part was really fun."

Miss Dalton turned her head toward the door. "Good morning, Ping," she said.

"Good morning," Ping replied as he put his book bag onto his desk.

"How are you this morning?" asked Miss Dalton.

"I am in good health," answered Ping. Quickly he opened his English vocabulary book and held it up in front of his face.

"You want me to drill you on the words?" asked Katie. She walked over to Ping's desk and took the book out of his hand. "I'll tell you a word, and you tell me the definition."

Katie turned to Lesson 1. "The first word is caricature. What does caricature mean?"

"Caricature mean grotesque or ludicrous exaggeration," replied Ping.

"Good work! That's exactly right. How about symbolism? What does symbolism mean?"

"Symbolism mean art of symbol to reveal or suggest intangible truth." Katie went through the list of vocabulary words—and each time Ping answered correctly.

"Wow! You really learned these words by heart." Katie handed the book back to Ping and sat down at her desk.

What would Mr. Cherry think if a kid who hardly spoke English got a better grade than she did? She opened her vocabulary book, put an index card over the definitions, and reviewed each word again.

Katie looked up each time a student entered the classroom, waiting to catch Spud's attention. Brian came in wearing another rock T-shirt. This one was purple, with a guy playing a burning black electric guitar. Brian wore his usual dark glasses, even though it was raining outside. His long, black hair stayed curly when it was wet.

When Spud strolled in, Katie tossed her hair over her shoulder and adjusted the front of her sundress. Before Spud took his seat in the back row, he hummed three notes loudly. Katie remembered what Spud had said during lunch the day before: Everyone was supposed to start humming at 9:15 in English class. She noticed that Spud was wearing white tennis shorts and a T-shirt that said "Surf's Up." He had a woven rope bracelet on his left wrist.

"Good morning, boys and girls," said Miss Dalton. She stood in front of her desk, took off her glasses, and rang her brass bell. "Please rise for the Pledge of Allegiance."

After the pledge, Miss Dalton scanned the G.W. daily bulletin. "The principal, Dr. Ward, has asked me to announce that we will be choosing the editorial staff for the *Golden Plume* literary magazine soon. All G.W. students in grades seven, eight, and nine are invited to submit material. The editorial board will consist of two faculty members—I'm happy to say I am one of them—and five students from each grade level. We will meet ninth period every Wednesday. I'd be delighted to have some of my homeroom students in the group. Does this sound of interest to any of you?"

Katie looked around the room. Meghan, Bambi Talbot, and Brian raised their hands.

"Brian, I understand you've already been published."

"I once had a short story published in *The London Gazette*," he said. "I'm more interested in writing poetry at the moment." Katie noticed that Brian had a Lucite pencil case with a gold clasp.

"That's wonderful," said Miss Dalton, smiling broadly. "I certainly hope you'll submit some poems for consideration. We have a fine tradition of excellence in creative writing here at G.W."

"I could submit some dirty jokes," Spud said in a serious voice. The back row snickered.

"How about a clever cartoon instead, Spud?" suggested Miss Dalton as she walked behind her desk. "I'd also like to remind everyone that the first J.V. football game of the season is today after school. I certainly hope all of you plan to attend."

Katie knew that Spud had made first string on the G.W. junior varsity football team, even though he was in the seventh grade. Once she had tried out for the cheerleading squad in sixth grade, only she had kicked left while the rest of the girls had kicked right. She didn't make the squad.

When the bell rang to end homeroom, Katie quickly grabbed her book bag and followed Spud down the hall. Spud would know which stairwell to take to first-period English.

Mr. Cherry pulled a map down over the front blackboard as Katie followed Spud into the classroom. Today Spud smelled of pine-scented cologne. She sat down next to Meghan and studied her vocabulary words. It was a bad sign when a map was pulled down over the front blackboard. It usually meant a pop quiz.

Mr. Cherry unbuttoned his tweed jacket and stood in front of the class. "Let's begin our lesson today with a little quiz on the vocabulary words from Lesson 1," he said, scratching his beard. "After we correct the quiz, I'd like to continue our discussion of *The Tell-Tale Heart*. Did you enjoy rereading the story last night for homework?"

"I think the story is brilliant," said Brian.

"Edgar Allan Poe is the quintessential short-story writer," said Mr. Cherry, "particularly when it comes to the art of creating foreshadowing, tension, and climax."

"What does quintessential mean?" Katie whispered to Meghan.

Meghan whispered back, "I think it means real good." Katie nodded in agreement.

"Now, I'd like you to please take out a white sheet of notebook paper. Put your name, date, and period number in the upper right-hand corner and number the lines to twenty in the margin on the left side, skipping a space between each number."

"Could you please repeat that?" asked Katie, raising her hand.

Mr. Cherry repeated the directions. Katie felt the heat coming up into her cheeks. All she could remember was to put her name and date in the right—or was it the left—

hand corner. She looked over at Meghan's paper and copied exactly what Meghan had written.

The vocabulary test was multiple choice. Katie knew that if she copied carefully from the board, she wouldn't have to worry about her spelling. She checked each word by saying the letters quietly out loud under her breath. She scanned the page for letter reversals, particularly "b's" and "d's," and then looked up at Mr. Cherry. Only one other boy was still working on the test. He'd come to class without a pencil. Mr. Cherry had allowed him to choose a pencil from his large collection in the drawer.

"Please exchange your paper with the person sitting to your left," said Mr. Cherry.

Katie handed her paper to Meghan. "Your *left*," whispered Meghan, handing the paper back to Katie. Katie gave her paper to Elroy Flowers, a boy she'd known in sixth grade. He had a comic book hidden inside his anthology.

As Mr. Cherry reviewed each definition, Katie corrected Meghan's paper. Meghan only got two words wrong, so Katie put a large "90 %" and a smiling face at the top of her page.

Elroy handed Katie her paper. It had "70 %" written across the top. *At least I passed*, Katie thought with relief. Mr. Cherry stood in front of the class and adjusted his bow tie.

"When I announce your name, please read me your score so I can record it in my grade book." Katie glanced at the kids sitting behind her. Nina looked relaxed, but Spud made a face as if he'd just been stung by a bee.

"Meghan."

"90%."

"Katie."

"70%."

"Elroy."

"85%."

"Brian."

"100%."

"Ping."

"100%."

"Spud."

"65%."

"Nina."

"85%."

At the end of the roll, Mr. Cherry asked Ping to stand up.

"Isn't it odd, young man," he said, "that there are two perfect papers in this class, and the two perfect scores are sitting next to each other? Doesn't that strike you as quite a coincidence?"

"Coincidence," said Ping, nodding his head.

"Ping, did you copy from Brian's paper? Is this quiz your own work?"

"Own work," said Ping, smiling and nodding his head.

"I find that hard to believe." Mr. Cherry squinted his beady gerbil eyes.

"Excuse me, Mr. Cherry," interrupted Katie, her heart hammering. "I know that Ping knew these words by heart."

"And what business is this of yours, Miss Kelso?" asked Mr. Cherry, peering down at her over his horn-rimmed glasses.

"Well, I drilled him in homeroom. I swear he knew every single word."

"That will be enough of this discussion," said Mr. Cherry, closing his grade book. "I must warn you that cheating is regarded as a very serious offense here at G.W. Is that clear?" Mr. Cherry buttoned his tweed jacket and picked up his worn copy of the English anthology. "Now, let us all turn to page 18 and *The Tell-Tale Heart*."

As the discussion began, Katie was distracted by a low murmur from the back row. She glanced at the clock. It was 9:13. Elroy began to hum in a deep, low monotone. Mr. Cherry continued with the discussion. The hum grew louder. Katie glanced behind her. Spud and his friends in the back row were taking notes and looking up intently at Mr. Cherry. Spud's lips were closed, but Katie could see his Adam's apple moving up and down.

Suddenly Mr. Cherry slammed his anthology down on the desk. Katie jumped. "Who is responsible for this juvenile behavior?" he demanded. "I refuse to continue teaching until there is utter silence in this classroom." The hum ceased. Mr. Cherry's hands were shaking and there was perspiration in little drops on his forehead.

"Now, let us continue like ladies and gentlemen," he said calmly. "As I was saying, how did the author use foreshadowing to heighten the dramatic tension?"

A high-pitched drone rose up again from the back row. Katie heard Elroy's horsefly-buzzing sound grow louder.

She cringed. What if Mr. Cherry had a heart attack or went insane right there in the classroom? She suddenly felt sorry for Mr. Cherry. He looked pitiful, standing there in front of the class with perspiration dripping down onto his starched white collar.

"This class has a choice," said Mr. Cherry, his voice quivering. "You can return at 7 a.m. on Monday morning to continue this discussion, or we can complete our discussion now. What will it be?"

Spud tipped back in his chair and raised his hand. "This is a cool story," he said, smiling at Mr. Cherry. "I like how Mr. Poe gets us in the mood. I vote we continue our discussion now." Every student in the class nodded in agreement. When the bell rang to end the first period, Mr. Cherry took the clean white handkerchief out of his jacket pocket and wiped his forehead.

"Class dismissed," he said, sounding relieved.

Katie closed her three-ring binder and stood up to walk to the Learning Center. On Fridays she had math seventh period instead of second period so she could go to the Learning Center. She liked it there. The teachers helped kids with their tests and homework. They understood about learning differences. Katie saw that Brian was waiting. He slouched by the classroom door, his leather book bag slung over his right shoulder.

"I like what you did," he said.

"What do you mean?" asked Katie.

"The way you stood up for Ping in class. I don't think he cheated either."

"I think it was cruel of Mr. Cherry to accuse Ping of cheating like that in front of the whole class," said Katie. "Poor kid can hardly speak English, and Cherry puts him down for studying harder than anyone else. Except you, that is," she added.

"I already knew those words," said Brian, almost apologetically. "I rarely ever have to study."

"So Katie's still in love with the Chink," teased Spud, walking out the classroom door.

"I'd better get to class," said Katie, throwing a disgusted look at Spud.

"What class do you have next?" asked Brian.

Katie didn't want to tell Brian that she was going to the Learning Center. "I'm going to math," she said. "Math is pretty easy for me, except when we have to memorize advanced formulas."

"Have a good weekend," said Brian, putting on his dark glasses. He acted and talked more like a ninth grader. Katie liked the way Brian's curly hair almost touched his shoulders.

"You too," said Katie. She watched as Brian took long strides down the hall. He was tall, as tall as Spud, but he walked in an awkward way, almost as if one leg was slightly shorter than the other.

CHAPTER

The Learning Center was on the second floor, next to the school library. Katie walked in and sat down at a table next to Mrs. Chandler.

"You've got to help me with my paragraph about the Pilgrims," she said right away. "It's due next period. I tried to write it last night, but my mind went blank." Katie was tempted to ask Mrs. Chandler about her seashell earrings, but she didn't want to get her off the subject until her paragraph was written.

"Katie, what exactly is your assignment?" asked Mrs. Chandler, picking up a yellow pad of paper.

"Mr. Lopez wants us to write about the first Thanksgiving, using authentic details."

"Can you draw on any personal experience?"

"I'm not a Pilgrim! How can I draw on personal experience?"

47

"Have you ever been really cold? I mean cold to the bone?" asked Mrs. Chandler.

"Yeah, sure, lots of times."

"Tell me about it."

"Well, once on Nantucket, in the winter, we went skating on Hummock Pond and I got so cold the inside of my nose froze. It hurt to breathe."

"Have you ever been really hungry?" asked Mrs. Chandler.

"Once Dad and I went on a camping trip and Mom forgot to put the pack with all the food in the car. When we hiked into the cabin, we had nothing to eat except instant coffee and bouillon cubes left there over the winter. I went to bed starving."

"Katie, you tell stories with good expression and detail. How would it be if you talked into a tape recorder before we try to get your ideas down on paper? Could you imagine what a girl your age might be feeling on the first Thanksgiving in Plymouth?"

"She'd be happy to worship God and not to be massacred by the Indians or eaten alive by a wild bear, or left without a roof over her head on bitter cold winter nights."

"You once told me you like to write in a diary," said Mrs. Chandler.

"How about if I write a page of a diary from a Pilgrim girl?" asked Katie excitedly.

Mrs. Chandler nodded. "That would be a very creative way to approach this assignment."

"I'll pretend that there is a Pilgrim girl named Abigail Warren who is trying to get the attention of a Pilgrim boy named Nathaniel Abbott. Abigail will be cutting up a turkey and carrots and herbs to make a turkey stew. Her fingers are so numb in the November frost that the knife slips and she cuts her finger. It begins to bleed. Nathaniel is sharpening arrowheads for his friend Gurgling Brook the Indian, and he rushes over to help Abigail. They both kneel down and give prayers to God that the finger has not been cut off completely, and they pray it will heal without disease."

"You've got the idea, Katie. Go over to that table and talk your story into the tape machine. After you've come up with the major ideas, we can organize your thoughts into a logical sequence."

"This is fun," said Katie, picking up the tape recorder. "I never thought I'd say that about a social studies writing assignment!"

By the time the bell rang to end second period, Katie had written a topic sentence, five sentences with supporting details, and a concluding "echo" sentence. She asked Mrs. Chandler to help her proofread the paper for spelling errors. Even using her best handwriting, the page looked sloppy. Katie wished she had time to put her paragraph on the word processor. Then Mr. Lopez would be really impressed. He might even read her diary page aloud to the entire class.

During social studies class, Katie felt a sense of pride as she handed Mr. Lopez her homework assignment. She wished that she could go to the Learning Center more often. The teachers there really helped to get her good ideas down on paper. They knew how to make you feel smart even if you couldn't spell, or write neatly, or read as smoothly as an announcer on TV.

After third period, Katie looked for Corky in the cafeteria. She saw Ping sitting alone at a table. She considered joining him for lunch but changed her mind. No P.K.'s would sit at that table. If Spud caught her eating alone with Ping, he'd tease her for the rest of the year. He might not ever ask her out on a date. Katie spotted Corky.

"How was your morning?" she called as she hurried past Ping's table on the way to her friend.

Corky didn't look up. She was studying for her first French quiz. "*Fermez la bouche,*" she said, chewing on a French fry.

"What's that mean?" asked Katie, pulling up a chair.

"It means, 'Close your mouth,' or as we say in America, 'Shut up'!" Katie looked startled. "I don't mean to be rude," explained Corky, "but I've got to learn all these verbs and vocabulary words by sixth period. I just started studying for the quiz about ten minutes ago." Corky took out her pencil and began to conjugate the verb "to be."

"I can't believe you can memorize so many words by studying just two periods before a test."

Corky looked distracted. "This mechanical pencil is driving me nuts," she said, violently twisting the eraser end of the pencil. "I can't seem to get it to work right."

"Let me see that," said Katie, taking the pencil. "The lead is just stuck." She shook the pencil up and down a few times. "It just needed a little loosening up."

"You can fix anything," Corky said, looking impressed.

"Spud got us in real trouble in Pit's English class," Katie said, chewing on one of Corky's French fries. "We almost had early morning detention."

"What did he do?"

"He made us hum."

"Sounds drastic," said Corky, picking up her vocabulary list. "I found out that guy Brian is some sort of a genius. He's in advanced-placement math."

"Not only that," added Katie, "in homeroom he said he'd published a story in some magazine. I think it won a prize."

"No kidding." Corky stuffed a huge bite of hamburger into her mouth. "Don't you think Brian needs a haircut?" she said with her mouth full.

"I like his hair. He's different looking," said Katie. "He seems like a loner. I don't think he's made any friends."

"Teachers will love him even if kids don't," said Corky. She put down her chocolate milk and fluffed up her short curly hair as Spud walked over to their table.

"What's up, dude?" Spud stood behind Katie and gave her long hair a tug.

"Ouch," said Katie. "Stop pulling my hair."

"Oh, poor baby," said Spud. "Are you going to the seventh-grade dance next Friday night?"

"I might think about it," said Katie, tossing her hair over her shoulder.

"You going with Porkie, here? You two could go together and be Beauty and the Beast."

"Don't call my friend Porkie," said Katie.

"Pardon me, sweetie pie," said Spud, taking two steps backward. "I didn't intend to offend Miss Beauty. I will leave you here to dine in peace with Miss Beast." He turned his back and walked over to take a bite out of Mary Ruth's orange Popsicle.

"That guy's getting on my nerves," said Katie. "Just because he's cute he thinks he can get away with being a jerk."

"Yes, but didn't it sound like he was asking you out?" asked Corky, swallowing her milk with a gulp.

"You think so, really?" Katie asked excitedly. "He just wanted to know if I was going to the dance, that's all."

"Sounds to me like he was asking you out," said Corky. She picked up her French vocabulary list. "I left my glasses at home," she said squinting. "I can hardly see these words."

"Want me to read them to you?" offered Katie.

"You can't read English, let alone French," Corky said impatiently. "You better leave me alone. I've got to study."

Katie stood up abruptly and walked away from the table. She didn't even say good-bye.

"Thanks anyway," called Corky after her, but Katie didn't turn around. She hoped Corky realized that she had hurt her feelings. Ping waved shyly as Katie passed his table. She checked to see if Spud was watching. "Hi, Ping," she almost whispered as she hurried by his table without stopping.

On the way home from school, Katie stopped at the drugstore to buy dusty-rose eye shadow with her baby-sitting money.

"What beautiful eyes you have," said the lady behind the counter. She had stiff blue hair that looked frozen in place.

"Thank you," said Katie. People had raved about her eyes ever since she could remember. "You have pretty eyes, too."

The lady looked up, surprised. "Thank you, dear," she said, with a wistful expression. "It's been a long time since I've had a compliment."

Katie pictured the lady sitting in a stuffed chair watching TV and eating a microwave dinner all alone. "I hope you have a good weekend," Katie called cheerfully as she left the store.

When Katie arrived home, she found her mother sitting alone at the kitchen table. It was rare to see her mother sitting down. Usually she was rushing to a meeting, practicing for a rehearsal, or doing a load of laundry.

"Welcome home, Kate. How did your English vocabulary test go?"

"How did you know we were going to have a quiz?"

"Teachers love to give quizzes on Fridays. When I taught music before your Dad and I were married, I always gave tests on Friday. That way you have the weekend to correct the papers."

"I got a 70 percent," said Katie, dropping her heavy book bag.

"Well, it could be worse," her mother sighed. "At least you passed. Next week we will start to review the words on Monday night instead of putting it off until Thursday."

"Can I have a sleep-over tonight?"

"Kate, love, I have to ask you to baby-sit again. I'm sorry, honey, but this is important."

"Give me a break," said Katie, slamming down her English anthology. "I've had enough of this baby-sitting. I want my own life. I feel like a live-in servant."

"I have a doctor's appointment. The only time she could see me was 6:30 tonight and your dad is running late again at the office."

"Are you sick? You don't look sick to me."

"No, I'm not sick. I found a lump in my breast. It is probably nothing, just a cyst, but I need to get it checked out."

"What time will you get home?" asked Katie. "Maybe Corky could come for a sleep-over after you get back from the doctor."

"We'll see what time it is when I get home." Her mother wound wisps of reddish hair into the bun on top of her head. She had on Katie's favorite gold hoop earrings. "You can feed the boys tuna salad, milk, and carrot sticks for supper. We have fresh fruit or chocolate ice cream for dessert."

"A real gourmet delight," Katie grumbled, beginning to set the table. "Where are the little darlings?"

"Sam is playing with Paul and Robbie. He'll be home at six. Willy is in the living room watching 'Sesame Street.' He'll need a bath right after dinner."

"I'm going up to my room," Katie muttered. "Tell me before you leave." Katie glanced at her mother standing in front of the kitchen sink. She was staring out the kitchen window as if her thoughts were as far away as the moon.

"What did you say, dear?"

"I said, 'Call me before you leave.'" Katie carried her book bag up the stairs to her room. She closed the door, lay down on her bed, and reached for her radio. She began searching for a station because she wasn't in the mood for all-rock, all-the-time. Something even louder would be better. She wished she could remember the numbers of her favorite stations. Katie kept rotating the dial until she heard an announcer's familiar voice. Then she turned up the volume and lay back on her pillow.

"Telephone," her mother screamed up the stairs. Katie ran into her parents' bedroom and picked up the phone.

"Hello," she said.

"Katie, why didn't you call? I've been waiting for you to call for hours." Katie could tell Corky was chewing on something hard, like a Life Savers candy.

"I just got home," said Katie coldly.

"Look, I'm sorry that I snapped at you at lunchtime. I was really uptight about my French class."

Katie felt relieved that Corky had apologized. "That's okay," she said. "How did you do on the quiz?"

"It was a cinch. I think I got every verb correct even though some kids dropped a bunch of marbles at 12:45 and it wasn't easy to concentrate. Want to go to the movies tonight? My mom says she'll drive us. Lots of kids are going. We can sit in the back row like we did for *Murder on Main Street, Part IV*."

"I can't."

"Why not?"

"I've got to baby-sit."

"Not again. You *always* have to baby-sit!"

"Tell me about it," said Katie in a disgusted tone. "If Mom isn't home too late, maybe you can come over for a sleep-over. I bought some new makeup we can try on."

"I'll call you, but I plan to hang out after the movies with Mary Ruth, Meghan, and Nina," said Corky.

"Have fun." Katie hung up the phone. She knew that Spud and his friends would be at the movies, especially the first Friday night after school started. They'd all be sitting in the front row eating freshly buttered popcorn. Spud would have his arm around a girl. If she were at the movies, he might sit right next to her and hold her hand in the dark.

At 6 p.m., Katie's mother knocked on her bedroom door. "I'm off," she said, opening the door. "I'll get back as soon as I can."

"Good luck, Mom," said Katie, turning off the radio. "I hope everything goes okay."

"You and me both!" Her mother blew Katie a kiss and hurried down the stairs. When Katie heard her mother's car back down the gravel driveway, she walked downstairs and turned off the TV. "Time for supper," she said.

Willy sat in his dad's leather chair, sucking his thumb. "Ice queem," he said, climbing down and following Katie into the kitchen.

"Where's Mom?" asked Sam, walking in the back door just as Katie finished piling tuna fish onto slices of bread. Willy was in his high chair, waiting expectantly.

"She's gone to the doctor."

"Not you again. Are you baby-sitting?"

"What does it look like I'm doing, going to a prom?"

Sam looked annoyed. "Where's Dad? I need him to fix my bike."

"Dad's late again, as usual," Katie said irritably. "What's wrong with your bike?"

"Ice queem," whined Willy.

"Something's wrong with the brakes."

"I'll look at it after supper."

"Ice queem!" shrieked Willy, pounding the tray of his high chair.

"Here!" Katie plopped a scoop of chocolate ice cream on top of Willy's tuna fish. "Now be quiet and eat your supper."

Willy held his spoon in his left hand and took a big bite of ice cream and tuna fish.

Sam jumped up from the table when he heard his father's car coming up the gravel driveway. Mr. Kelso worked in Boston as the program director of Channel 2, a local TV station. Sometimes it took him more than an hour to get home from the city, especially on a Friday night.

"Down," cried Willy, tugging at the dish towel around his neck. Katie lifted Willy out of his high chair. He ran to hug his dad's pant leg, leaving a blob of ice cream on his pin-striped blue suit.

"Hi, kids," said Mr. Kelso, wiping the ice cream off his trousers with his handkerchief. "Who else has a kiss for your old dad?"

Sam gave his dad an affectionate punch in the stomach. Katie kissed her father on the cheek. She'd grown as tall as her dad's neck. She hoped she wouldn't grow up as tall as his chin. Then she'd be taller than every boy in her class, even Spud.

"Isn't your mother home from the doctor yet?" Her father looked concerned as he poured himself a drink.

"No, she left at six. She should be back any minute," answered Katie.

"Dad, will you help me fix my bike?" asked Sam. "Something's wrong with the hand brake."

"Let me change into my blue jeans," his father said. "I bet Katie can fix it. She knows more about fixing bikes than I do."

An hour later, Katie heard a car stop at the top of the driveway. She watched out the window as her mother slammed the car door and walked slowly toward the house. She was wearing her sunglasses, even though it was beginning to get dark.

Mrs. Kelso wearily opened the back screen door and walked into the kitchen. Mr. Kelso came in from the living room, an anxious look on his face. "Now can I call Corky for a sleep-over?" Katie asked, putting her arm around her mother's thin waist. "All my friends are going to the movies. If you drop me off, I can still make the first show."

"Katie, your Dad and I need to talk," her mother said in an unfamiliar voice. "I've decided to take him out to dinner. I need you to baby-sit until we get home. We won't be too late."

"You're kidding, Mom. You can't do this to me!" Katie cried.

"This is important, Kate," Mr. Kelso said. "You can go to the movies tomorrow."

"But all my friends are going tonight."

"Kate, please, let's not discuss it any further—What on earth is this?" Mrs. Kelso said, staring at Willy's chocolate tuna dish.

"A new recipe," Katie said angrily. "He loved it."

Her mother and father walked up the stairs without a word. They went into their bedroom and closed the door. When they came back down the stairs, they were holding hands.

"We won't be late," Mr. Kelso said. He looked worried, the way he did when he was about to go away on a business trip for longer than two nights.

"I want Mommy," howled Willy, following his parents to the back door. Tears rolled down his pink cheeks.

"Come with me, Willy, and I'll read you a story," Katie said. She picked Willy up, carried him into the living room, and sat him in her lap. She didn't mind reading to Willy. If she didn't know a word, she could substitute a word she did know. If a page had too much writing on it, she'd just make up a story by looking at the pictures. Willy loved to be read to. He forgot about his mother and father being gone. He sat quietly on Katie's lap and sucked his thumb as she read six books aloud.

After Katie put Willy into his crib for the night, she went outside to help Sam fix his bike. As she showed Sam how to tighten the hand brakes with the socket wrench, she remembered the time she'd figured out how to fix her parents' toilet so it would stop gurgling.

"This last twist should do it," Katie told Sam. She tested the brakes to make sure they worked properly.

"Thanks!" Sam said, buckling his bike helmet and hopping onto his purple mountain bike. He waved to Katie and rode down the driveway.

Katie washed the grease off her hands in the kitchen sink and went upstairs to check on Willy. Then she went into her bedroom and pulled her diary out from under the mattress. Unlocking the clasp with the secret combination, Katie took a pencil from her bedside table and began to write.

Deer Dairy,

Went to sckool. Mr. Pits said that Ping cheeted
but that wasn't true. He new all the voc. words by
hart. Spud made us hum at 9:15. Pit got really
upset but he was dum to say that Ping cheeted
when he didn't. Corky said in her French class kids
droped marbles at 12:45. Spud talked to me and
Corky at lunch. Sometimes he's mean like he calls
Corky, Porkie (she is pretty fat) and he calls Ping,
Wee Wee Dung. He might ask me out to the 7th
gr. danse. The new kid named Brain talked to me
to. He is shy with a thin face and long legs and
thick eyebrows but he is very smart. I fixed Sam's
dike. I can fix anything as long as I don't have to
read direcshons. Mom says that dislecktics are
good at fixing things. Mom is driving me Krazy.
She made me babysit <u>again</u>! It's not fair. She
bosses me around evry minut. I missed going to the
movies with Corky and all my freinds. I'll never get
to be a P.K. if I'm forced to babysit evry nite. I think
something is rong with Mom.

The End

CHAPTER

9

Mozart's bark woke Katie up on Saturday morning. The sun was streaming into her bedroom windows. Katie sat up in bed and smelled pancakes. Every Saturday, her father made the family thin Swedish pancakes for a late-morning breakfast. Katie put on shorts and a T-shirt and skipped down the stairs into the kitchen.

"Mozart, why were you barking?" she asked, nuzzling his head in her hands. Mozart wagged his tail and licked Katie's cheek.

"He was barking at a squirrel on the bird feeder," said Dad. "I'm glad you're up, Katie. There is something I'd like to discuss with all of you." He handed Katie a plate of piping hot pancakes.

Sam was already sitting at the kitchen table; Willy was in his high chair. They each had a tall stack of pancakes in front of them.

"Pass the syrup," said Sam.

"Please," reminded his father.

"Please pass the syrup," said Sam as he put a slab of butter between each pancake and poured a river of syrup over the top.

Katie's father poured himself another cup of black coffee and sat down at the table next to Willy.

"Where is Mom?" asked Katie, cutting Willy's pancakes into little bites.

"She's trying to sleep late. She had a rough day yesterday."

"What happened?" asked Sam.

Katie sensed that something was wrong. "Was it her doctor's appointment?" she asked.

Her dad nodded. "Your mother found a lump in her breast. Last night, the doctor told her she needs to go to the hospital for a biopsy."

"What's a biopsy?" asked Sam, taking a large bite of pancake.

"They'll study the cells from the lump under a microscope. If the cells look healthy, the doctor sends your mother home from the hospital the same day."

"What happens if the lump doesn't look healthy?" asked Katie.

"If there are cancer cells in the lump," her dad said, taking a deep breath, "then the doctors will help us decide what to do next."

"You mean Mom might have cancer?" asked Sam. He pushed away the rest of his pancakes.

"Possibly, but not necessarily. Chances are the lump is just a cyst. We'll know more on Friday. In the meantime, I want you kids to be especially helpful to your mother this week."

"More cakes," said Willy. Katie took a pancake off her plate and cut it into pieces for her brother.

"What about my birthday party?" asked Sam. "I'm supposed to have my birthday party on Saturday."

"Your mother and I discussed that last night. We've decided to rent Lucky Lanes bowling alley this Wednesday for your party. I'll take the afternoon off from work."

"And I suppose I'll have to baby-sit Willy," said Katie bitterly. She poked at her half-eaten pancakes and then put the plate onto the floor for Mozart.

"I'll bring you home some birthday cake," Sam said cheerfully. Her brother looked excited to be getting presents even sooner than he had expected.

"How long will Mom be in the hospital?" Katie asked.

"Hopefully, only one day. If she needs to be in the hospital longer, Aunt Susan and Uncle Ben and Simon and Josh will come over the weekend."

"You mean Simon and Josh are coming here?" Sam said eagerly. He loved to play army men with his cousins. "Can Josh sleep in my room?"

"We'll decide that when the time comes," said his father. He tapped his right foot on the floor. Katie noticed that whenever her father felt nervous, he always tapped his right foot.

"Katie fixed my bike. I'm going up to school to play kickball," Sam announced, clearing his place and bending down to pull up his socks. "I'll be home by lunchtime," he yelled as he ran out the door.

Mr. Kelso took another sip from his Channel 2 coffee mug. "How was your first week of school, Katie? We've hardly had a chance to talk."

"It's going all right, Dad. Corky is still my best friend, but I'm trying to make some new friends, like getting into the P.K. group."

"What's a P.K.?" asked her father.

"The P.K.'s are the popular kids. I've never been part of the 'in' group before. In junior high, I kind of want to get into a different crowd. Of course, I'll still be friends with Corky."

"I remember junior high as being quite difficult, at least socially," said her father.

"How old were you when you first started to date, Dad? Did you ever go out with a girl in the seventh grade?"

"As far as I can remember—and it's been awhile, you understand—in seventh grade we just went around together in groups. It wasn't until high school that I began to really date girls. I remember going steady with Harriet Simpson in my sophomore year."

"Things are different now, Dad. I'm pretty sure kids begin to date in the seventh grade. I plan to start going out with boys by Thanksgiving."

"I wish you luck," said her father, reaching over to hug his daughter. Katie could feel her dad had put on weight. "Only remember, you're my best girl, first and always."

"I know that, Dad," said Katie, giving her dad an affectionate punch on the arm. She wished her dad didn't have

65

to travel away from home so often. It seemed easier to talk to him than to her mother. Her mom just liked to tell her all the things she wasn't allowed to do. Her mom would probably try to stop her from dating, even after she fell in love.

On Saturdays, the teenagers in North Kent liked to hang out in front of Burger King or sit on the stone wall next to the drugstore. They played Hackey Sack or Frisbee in Longfellow Park. Now that Katie was in junior high, she was allowed to go to the park any time she wanted. She sensed it would be a good place to meet P.K.'s.

"Dad, can I have my allowance and all my baby-sitting money? I want to go downtown and meet my friends."

"How much do I owe you?"

Katie added on her fingers the $5 for allowance and the $4.50 for baby-sitting. She wished she had mastered her math facts better so she could add numbers quickly in her head.

"I think you owe me $9.50," she said, writing the numbers with a knife in the pancake flour.

"Here's $10," said her dad, taking a bill from his wallet. "Katie, you've been a real trouper about helping out with the boys this week. Your mom and I really appreciate all the baby-sitting you've done."

"Is Mom going to be okay?" Katie avoided looking her father directly in the eye.

"I certainly hope so," he replied, taking a long, deep breath. "All we can do at this point is hope and pray that the lump is not cancerous."

Katie nodded. She took Willy down from his high chair and carried him over to the sink. The front of his playsuit was sticky with syrup.

"I'll take care of Willy," said her father. "You go on downtown. And stay away from all those handsome boys."

"Yeah, I'll be beating them away with sticks." Katie handed Willy to her father and put the $10 bill in her pocketbook. She went into the bathroom and put powder and rose-red blush on her cheeks. She sprayed the ends of her hair with hair spray so they wouldn't get too frizzy in the humid air. Unzipping last year's pencil case, she chose "Hot Lips Pink" from her lipstick collection. Then she combed her hair so it swooped down over her left eye, like a movie star. Katie hurried to get out of the house before her mother woke up. If her mother saw her looking like this, she'd make her scrub her face with a washcloth and put her hair in a ponytail, or even worse, two braids.

"Good-bye, Dad," Katie called, running quickly out the front door. "I'm eating lunch downtown. I'll be home sometime this afternoon." She put her pocketbook strap over her shoulder as the screen door slammed behind her.

CHAPTER

10

Katie decided not to ride her bike downtown. The wind would blow her hair out of place when she glided down the Lincoln Avenue hill. Besides, she didn't want boys to see her with sweat stains under her arms. Instead, she strolled along the sidewalk toward Main Street. A car with five teenage boys inside honked at her as it sped past.

A crowd of kids from G.W. was sitting on the wooden bench outside of Burger King. Katie recognized Elroy Flowers, Mary Ruth, and Nina. Spud and Georgie were playing Hackey Sack.

"Want to play?" asked Spud, hitting the little beanbag sack into the air with his knee.

"I'll try," said Katie. "But I've never played Hackey Sack before." She swatted the Hackey Sack with her fist. It flopped over into the street and landed underneath a car.

"Sorry. I guess I need a little practice."

"You can say that again," said Georgie. He bent down and pushed the Hackey Sack out from under the car with a stick. Katie noticed Stephanie Ginsberg and Bambi Talbot coming up the street carrying Bloomingdale's shopping bags. Bambi had been a leader of the P.K.'s since fourth grade. She was class secretary and she went away to tennis camp in the summer.

"Hi, Bambi," said Katie. "Did you have a good summer?" Bambi's hair had a bleached-blond streak from the sun.

"Sure did. What about you?"

"I traveled a good deal," Katie exaggerated. "I went to the White Mountains and spent a week with Nana Kelso on Nantucket."

"Sounds cool." Bambi and Stephanie walked by Katie and sat down on the bench in front of Burger King. "I'm pooped," said Bambi.

"Me, too," said Stephanie. She took a comb and a mirror out of her purse. "My hair is a wreck," she moaned. She put a piece of bubble gum in her mouth and began to chew. "Want one?" she offered Bambi.

"No, thanks," said Bambi. "It gets stuck in my braces."

Katie looked across the street. She saw Brian sitting alone under a tree in Longfellow Park. He seemed to be writing something in a notebook.

"So where is your friend Porkie?" asked Spud, kicking the Hackey Sack high above his head. "I thought you two were inseparable."

"For your information, her name is Corky, not Porkie." Katie flipped her hair back and tried to think of a way to flatter Bambi.

"I like your pink sneakers," Katie said, looking down at Bambi's feet.

"Thanks. I have these same sneakers in four different colors. They're made in Japan. I like to color-coordinate my shoes with all my outfits."

"Katie loves things from Japan," said Spud, "especially boys like Wee Wee Dung, the Jap." He flipped the Hackey Sack into the air with the side of his foot. Bambi hit it back with the edge of her pink sneaker.

"Hey, Bambi, you're pretty good at this. You want to play Hackey Sack?" Spud asked.

"I'm too pooped," said Bambi. "Steffie and I have been shopping for hours."

Katie looked at their shopping bags. "What did you buy?" she asked.

"Just a few things for school. Steffie got a sweater with ducks on it. What do you think of Miss Dalton's homeroom?"

"It's okay, I guess," Katie replied.

"Do you still go to the Resource Room like you did last year?" Stephanie asked. "Don't you have some kind of learning problem?"

Katie nodded. "Yes, I have lysdexia. I mean dyslexia, but it's getting better, much better—I mean, I don't even need to go to the Resource Room anymore. I just get help now and then in the Learning Center."

"I go to the Learning Center myself," said Spud, kicking the Hackey Sack, "but only because it gets me out of taking a foreign language. How come I never see you there? You too busy making eyes at the Jap?"

"Knock it off, Spud," said Katie. "I'm not going out with Ping, and you know it. Besides, he's not a Jap, he's Chinese." Katie could feel her face turning red.

"Are you going out for cheerleading again this year?" asked Stephanie, blowing a bubble with her gum.

"I was considering it," said Katie. "When are the try-outs?"

"After school this Wednesday. The squad meets every Thursday in the gym to practice for the games."

"I may see you there," said Katie, backing down the street. She knew she had to baby-sit on Wednesday afternoon, and every Thursday she biked to her tutor on the other side of town.

Katie crossed the street and walked over to Brian. He had on leather sandals instead of the high-top sneakers that most seventh-grade boys wore. Brian took off his dark glasses as Katie walked over the freshly mowed lawn toward him.

"What are you doing, writing letters?" Katie asked. She could tell Brian was pleased to see her.

"I'm writing in my journal."

"I write in a diary every night," Katie said, sitting down beside him.

"Then you know the cathartic value of writing daily."

Katie wasn't sure what cathartic meant, but she gathered from Brian's tone of voice that something was on his mind.

"Where did you go to school last year?" she asked, crossing her legs comfortably on the grass.

"A boarding school outside of London."

Katie was impressed. "I've never been to Europe," she said with envy.

"I'm tired of going to upper-crust boys' boarding schools. I made Mother promise to send me to public school when the company transferred its headquarters to Boston."

"What does your father do?" Katie asked.

"My dad? Well, my dad is basically a beach bum. He lives on an island off Hawaii. Among other things, he writes trashy sex novels."

"No kidding!" said Katie.

"I don't live with my dad. I live with my mother and my stepfather, only my stepfather moved out, so now it's just my mother and myself."

"Just you and your mom live in that gigantic house?" asked Katie, surprised.

"How did you know I live in a gigantic house?"

"I noticed your address on my class list. Everyone knows the houses on Bella Vista are enormous."

"Actually, I've lived in mansions all my life, except for the time we had a ten-room apartment in Paris."

"Yikes! How did you get so rich?"

"My mother is a fashion designer. Have you ever heard of Lilly's Wrinkle Free women's apparel?"

"Yeah, sure. It's in all the department stores."

"Lilly is my mother."

Katie's mouth fell open. "Boy, she's really famous! You must be so proud of her."

Brian averted his eyes and looked down at the ground. He began to pull up pieces of grass and stack them in a pile on his journal.

"Actually, my mother is rarely home," he said. "She travels extensively on business. She's been gone since August 17th."

"Who takes care of you?"

"We've got a housekeeper and a cook, but my real friend is Oscar. He's the chauffeur. He lets me watch TV in his apartment. He and his wife have worked for us since I was six years old. Sometimes I get to sleep over on his pull-out couch. He likes to watch wrestling. Have you ever watched Mad Dog Watkins?"

"No. I hate wrestling. I always think they're killing each other."

"It's just an act. No one actually gets hurt."

"It's brutal, if you ask me," said Katie. "So, what do you think of Mr. Pits' English class?"

"Is that what the kids call him?" asked Brian, grinning.

"We either call him Mr. Pits or Cherry-Berry."

"I haven't talked to many kids," said Brian. "I haven't found too many seventh graders I can relate to."

Katie noticed Brian's digital watch. It flashed the time and date and had a tiny calculator on the side.

"Nice watch you've got," she said.

"Thanks. My mother brought this to me from Switzerland. If you press this button, it gives you the time in all the different time zones in the world." Brian pushed the button and announced that it was 3:40 a.m. in Australia.

"It must be really tough starting school in a new town in the seventh grade," said Katie.

"Making friends is never easy," he replied, "especially when you get bounced from one boarding school to another. Mother promised to stay in North Kent until I graduate from high school. Only now she's never home."

"I'd be really upset if I didn't have any friends," Katie said. "Corky has been my best friend since first grade. We know everything about each other."

"It may sound silly, but right now my best friend is this journal." Brian lay down on his side and rested his head on his elbow. He put a piece of tall grass in his mouth. "By the way, are you thinking of writing for the G.W. magazine?"

"Well, I hadn't really thought about it," said Katie.

"You like to write in your diary. This isn't much different, except it would be published."

"I'll have to think about it," said Katie.

"Miss Dalton talked to me about being one of the seventh-grade representatives. She wants me to submit some of my work to the editorial board."

"You must be a really good writer, especially since you've already been published," Katie replied. She was glad Brian didn't know anything about her learning difference.

"All you have to do is submit a writing sample," Brian continued, "and sign your name on the back of the page in pencil. Dr. Ward and Miss Dalton and the members of the present staff will read each submission. I think they plan to accept five seventh graders. Frankly, I often find that people who like to write are the most interesting. The *Golden Plume* magazine won't appeal to jerks, like that guy Spud in our English class."

Katie looked across the park. Spud was sitting between Bambi and Stephanie on the bench in front of Burger King. He had his arm around them both.

"Do you like to write poetry?" asked Brian, sensing her inattention.

"I write poetry, but it doesn't always rhyme," said Katie.

"What do you think of this?" Brian fumbled through the pages of his journal and pulled out a crumpled piece of white-lined paper.

Katie looked at the paper and read the first line, "Ode to Katie." She looked up amazed. "Is this about me?" she asked.

"I wrote that on Friday in math class. It needs to be polished. I haven't really finished it yet."

"No one has ever written me a poem before," said Katie, "especially a published author."

"I didn't really mean to show it to you," said Brian shyly. "Here, you read it. It isn't all that good."

Katie took the crumpled paper out of Brian's hand and began to read it aloud in a halting voice.

Ode to Katie

An Intelligent girl
So tall and slender,
For Ping in class
A valiant defender.

Katie's brown eyes
Like a Monarch dart,
She sees through my soul
And into My heart.

"Oh, Brian. This is beautiful! I don't know what to say."

"It still needs revision," Brian said, trying to act casual.

"But I'm really flattered you'd write something about me, especially since we just met."

"I feel pretty awkward about my wealth and all. I never know if kids are impressed by my famous parents or if they really care about me. You seem different. I feel I can trust you. I sense we have a lot in common."

"We both love to write," Katie agreed. "Can I keep this poem?"

Brian nodded. "Just don't show it to any of those jerks over in front of Burger King."

"Are you going to the seventh-grade dance next Friday night?" asked Katie, tucking the poem in her pocketbook.

"I doubt it," said Brian, looking down at his sandals. "In England we learned dances at school like the waltz and the fox-trot. I'm no good at American gyrations."

"Neither am I," Katie reassured him. "Don't worry. You don't have to dance. At the sixth-grade dances last year, we mostly ate pizza and just hung out. Some guys played Hackey Sack."

"I've never played Hackey Sack. The only sport I play is golf."

"Golf must be really fun," said Katie. "You can get an awesome tan on the golf course. . . . By the way, what time is it?"

Brian looked down at his digital watch. "Do you want to know the time in North Kent or Australia?" he joked.

"Let's try North Kent."

"It's five to twelve," said Brian.

"I better go." Katie stood up. "I'm meeting Corky for lunch."

"I enjoyed our conversation." Brian put on his dark glasses and brushed the dirt off his torn blue jeans. "I'll see you on Monday in school."

"Have a great weekend." Katie said, flipping her hair over her shoulder. She skipped over the grass toward the sidewalk. When she got to the street, she turned around and waved good-bye to Brian.

11

By the time Katie walked home from town, her mother had left for rehearsal. She saw her father sitting in his leather chair in the living room, watching football on TV. Willy was sitting in his lap, holding Ziz, his teddy bear.

"So, did you pick up any handsome men?" asked her father as she walked in.

"Not exactly," said Katie. "But I'm going to a dance next Friday night. It's our first seventh-grade recreation night at school."

"That sounds like fun. Did you find Corky? She called here twice after you left."

"We ate lunch at Burger King. Dad, I talked to this really interesting new guy named Brian. He's lived all over the world. His dad writes best-sellers in Hawaii, and his mother is Lilly, the fashion designer. He's really brilliant. He's in advanced math, and he published a story in a magazine in England. He even wrote me a poem called 'Ode to Katie.'" Katie took a wrinkled piece of paper out of her pocketbook and handed the poem to her father. "Look at this!" she said proudly.

"This kid appears quite talented," her father remarked as he read Brian's poem.

"He's in Cherry's English class. You won't believe this, but he wants me to try out for the G.W. literary magazine."

Her dad looked pleased. "I wrote for a literary magazine once myself," he said, shifting Willy to his other knee. "I actually had several essays published. I think I even saved a few copies of the magazines."

"That's impressive, Dad. I didn't know you could write. Can I see the magazines?"

"I hope your mother didn't throw them out," said her father, putting Willy on the floor. "She's always trying to clean up the cellar."

Katie and Willy followed their father down the cellar stairs. Her dad opened a cardboard box. It was full of old yearbooks and term papers.

"I wrote these papers in college," he said proudly, flipping through a folder of term papers. "In a way, your mother and I met because of these philosophy papers."

"What do you mean?" asked Katie.

"Your mother was taking a course in logic. She was about to fail the course."

"Mom was about to fail a course?" Katie asked excitedly.

"She was a good student in college, but as hard as she tried, she just couldn't seem to grasp logical principles. She's a very intuitive thinker, your mother."

"What do you mean, Dad?"

"Well, for example, suppose I said, 'Some people with blue eyes have blond hair. All people with blond hair are right-handed. Some people with blue eyes are right-handed. Is that true or false?'"

"I don't get it," said Katie.

"Neither did your mother," her father replied. "You see, I was majoring in philosophy at the time. The professor knew I was on a scholarship and needed money, so he asked if I'd be interested in tutoring a freshman who was having trouble passing the logic course. The next thing I knew, in the door walks your mother."

"Was it love at first sight?"

"Well, not exactly. You see, I was intrigued because I'd never met a woman with a mind like your mother's. She has what they call an artistic temperament. She's the type who will buy an electric toaster on a whim because she likes the color. I, on the other hand, would never purchase an appliance without first researching it in *Consumer Reports* magazine."

"I think I'm like Mom. I like to follow my feelings."

"Both you and your mother are amazingly sensitive and intuitive women. At times, I think I'm living with a pair of mind readers."

"I'm also a good artist, just like Mom. Remember last year when Mr. Carroll put my self-portrait on the front bulletin board at Ridge School?"

Her father nodded. "You're like your mother in many ways."

"Like what, Dad?" asked Katie, thumbing through his senior yearbook.

"Neither one of you can spell worth beans. My advice to you, Katie, is to marry a man who can spell."

"Don't worry, Dad. Mom already told me that. She also told me to marry a man who can read a map. I get lost just like Mom, and I don't even have my license."

"Look at this. I think I found it!" Her father pulled a gold and black booklet out from the bottom of the box. "Let's see if I had anything published in this issue." Her father turned to the index. "See, look at this. 'The Examination of Metacognition,' by Jack Fenwick Kelso."

Katie took the magazine and thumbed through the pages. "Can I borrow this, Dad? I'd like to read some of the poetry."

"Don't you want to read my essay on metacognition?" he teased.

"It's pretty long, Dad," said Katie. "But I'll give it a try."

Willy walked over with a Christmas tree bulb in his teeth.

"Where did you find that, Willy?" asked his father, taking the bulb out of his mouth.

"Oh, no!" Katie cried. "Look what Willy's done! He's put all the Christmas tree decorations into the clothes dryer."

Her dad took Willy by the hand. "You can't let this child out of your sight for one minute," he said. Katie and her father began to wrap each bulb back into aged tissue paper. They packed up the Christmas tree decorations and closed the box marked "J.F.K. College Storage."

"I'm going upstairs to listen to music," said Katie. "What time is supper?"

"I'm tired of cooking, and I'm not brave enough to take Willy to a restaurant, not after he spilled the beer in my lap the last time we went out. Let's order Chinese food and have it delivered."

"Great idea. Order an egg roll and fried rice for me."

Katie ran up the stairs and climbed onto her bed. She reached down and took her diary out from under the mattress.

Setp. 12

Deer Dairy,

Today is Saterday, no sckool. I put on eye make-up and lipstick and got out of the house before Mom cot me. I hung out with P.K.'s in front of Berger king. Spud the Stud was there. He goes to the L. Center too. He tries to act so cool and all the grils adoor him. He's a supper athleet. I started to make freinds with Bambee. She's a P.K. I talked to Brain from Pit's class. Corky thinks he's weerd but I think he's sensative to people's feelings. He seems reely lonely. He's got sad brown eyes and longish black curlie hair and he's taller than I am. He rote me a

pome. I showed the pome to Dad and Dad said
Brian is excepshionly talented. Brian wants me to
be on the lit. mag. in sckool. Brian doen't know
about my dislexia. I think he thinks I am a brian.
Dad says Mom and I think alike. We read poeple's
minds. Mom has to go to the hostible for a
byopsee test. Willy put the Xmas decorashions in
the drier. He's cute but he's a pain to take care of.
Brian hardly sees his parents. His dad lives in
Ha-y-ee and his mom travels. I can't beleive she
wasn't at home for the 1st week of sckool. I feel
sorry for Brian. He says his showfur is real nice
thow. Tonight I don't have to babysit. I'm going to
the movies with Corky. I hope P.K.'s will be there
esp. Spud. Corky doesn't want to be a P.K. but I
do. I'm going to make freinds with Stefanie and
Bambee no matter what Corky thinks. She's such
a brain she doesn't need new freinds like I do. She
probly won't even get a boy freind in 7th gr.

The End

CHAPTER

12

The Monday afternoon sun beat down on the front steps of George Washington Junior High. Katie rolled up the sleeves of her cotton dress to renew her summer tan. She squinted her eyes and watched the students file from the dark G.W. hallways into the bright sunlight.

Dominique Rousseau pushed open the heavy G.W. front door. She was an eighth grader who lived on Front Street next to Katie. Her father worked for Renault cars and had been transferred from the Paris office to the Boston office. When Dominique saw Katie, she walked over and sat down on the steps beside her.

"Hi, Katie," she said with a slight French accent. "I sit next to a boy named Brian in my math class and he said you might be interested in being on the editorial staff of the *Plume*."

Katie squinted at Dominique. "I'm giving it some thought," she said, holding her hand over her eyes like a visor. "I'm not sure if I have enough time to be on the literary staff this year."

"It's really fun," said Dominique. "I was on the staff last year. I made tons of new friends."

"Did you have a good summer?" Katie tried to change the subject.

"I had a great summer. First we went to Paris for a week to visit my relatives. Then my parents and my grandmother and I drove down to the Riviera. We spent two weeks in St. Tropez."

Spud walked by and sat down next to Katie. He flexed the muscles in his upper arm and put his hand on her shoulder.

"What's up, dude?" he asked, giving her shoulder a squeeze.

"Dominique went to the Riviera this summer," said Katie, unsure of how to react to his arm on her shoulder.

"Did you see any nude bathers?" asked Spud. "I hear French women go around topless."

"Sometimes you see topless bathers at the beach," said Dominique. "No one pays much attention to them."

"Man, I'd pay attention," said Spud, grinning.

Katie blushed. She pictured herself walking along the beach holding hands with Spud and meeting a topless French lady.

"So, are you coming to the dance on Friday night, sweetie pie?" Spud gave her arm another squeeze. "I'll be waiting for you." Spud winked at Katie. Then he stood up and jumped down the G.W. steps two at a time.

"He's cute," said Dominique. "What's his name?"

"His name is Spud. Or at least that's what kids call him."

"Is he the guy Brian thinks is such a jerk?"

"Sometimes Spud can get on your nerves," Katie admitted. "Is Brian a friend of yours?"

"He's in my advanced math class. All I know is, he's *tres intelligent*. One day Oliver Feeney asked a question the teacher couldn't figure out, and Brian explained the answer to the whole class."

"He's really good in English, too," said Katie. "He writes poetry all the time."

Dominique stood up and stretched. "I've got to go to my ballet class," she said. "Maybe I'll see you at the literary club meetings."

"That would be great," said Katie. She stood up and straightened her dress. It was getting too hot to sit any longer in the direct sun. Katie walked down the G.W. steps and sat down in the shade of the maple tree. A giant bug clinging to the bark caught her attention.

"That's just a cicada," said a voice behind her, "the kind of insect you hear serenading on long and sultry summer nights." Brian dropped his brown leather book bag and sat down beside her.

"But it's huge!" Katie poked the bug with a stick. "How come it isn't making any noise? Do you think it's asleep?"

"Actually, the male emits no sound from its mouth," Brian explained. "The male cicada makes a peculiar buzzing sound with membranes which are inside the abdomen. That shrill monotone sound is actually a mating call."

"How do you know so much about cicada bugs?" asked Katie.

"I've collected insects for years," said Brian. "I am also an amateur lepidopterist."

"What on earth is that?"

"I collect butterflies. The last time I visited my father in Hawaii, I netted a Killima."

"I love butterflies," said Katie, throwing back her hair.

"I've got over a hundred different species," said Brian proudly. "Would you like to see them sometime?"

"You mean at your house?"

"Sure. You could come over and see my B and B collection—B and B, for bugs and butterflies."

"I'd love to come see it," said Katie excitedly.

"How about on Wednesday after school?" asked Brian.

"No, I can't come on Wednesday because I have to baby-sit my little brother Willy."

"How about Thursday afternoon?"

Katie shook her head. "No, I have an appointment," she said, "a doctor's appointment." She did not want to tell Brian that she went to a tutor every Thursday afternoon.

"Well, how about today?" asked Brian

"You mean right now, this afternoon?"

"Why not? We could walk home to my house together."

"But I've got a lot of homework," said Katie hesitantly.

"Maybe my driver could give you a lift back home. Oscar wouldn't mind. He's getting really bored with my mother gone." Brian looked at her persuasively. "What do you say?"

"I'll have to call my mom to ask permission."

"No problem. I'll wait here while you go call."

When Katie returned from telephoning, she skipped down the G.W. steps. "My mom says to be home by five," she called excitedly. Katie slung her book bag over her shoulder and followed Brian to Bella Vista Drive.

As they walked up the sidewalk to the crest of the hill, Katie stopped to admire a view of the entire Boston skyline.

"There's the house," said Brian, pointing to a stately three-story brick mansion. Katie's eyes scanned a perfectly manicured lawn that stretched the length of several football fields. "Who cuts all this grass?" she panted, rubbing her calf.

"We have a full-time gardener who takes care of the swimming pool, tennis courts, and all the grounds. Since we just got here in August, Ralph won't be able to plant the vegetable garden until next spring."

Katie looked over at the four-car garage. "You must have a lot of cars," she said.

"Oscar drives the limo. Mother drives the Ferrari. My stepfather used to have a Porsche and a Mercedes station wagon before he moved out. Now we put the lawn mower tractor in the Porsche space."

Brian took a key out of his Lucite pencil case and unlocked the side door of the house. He held the screen door open for Katie.

"We never use the front door. It's so formal walking up all those brick steps and under the marble arch. I prefer the kitchen door myself, but I use this one, the side door, with guests. Actually, you're the first guest I've had," Brian added shyly.

"This is awesome!" Katie drew in her breath. She gazed at a living room the size of the school cafeteria. It had red velvet wallpaper and two crystal chandeliers hanging from the ceiling. "I've never seen a room like this, except in magazines. Your mom has exquisite taste."

"My mother didn't do this. She's never had time to take care of the house. Mother hired a decorator to come up from New York. He worked on the house for five months before we moved in. By the time we got here in August, all the boxes were unpacked and the place was in perfect order."

A lady dressed in a gray uniform with a lace apron around her waist walked into the living room.

"Miss Gumpert, I'd like you to meet my friend, Katie."

"How do you do," said Katie. She used the little curtsy she had learned in dancing school. Miss Gumpert smiled. Her lips were tight and pencil-thin.

"Katie goes to G.W. with me. She is also a writer."

"And I like butterflies," added Katie.

"I brought her to see my B and B collection," Brian explained.

"I don't think your mother would approve of taking a young lady alone into your bedroom," replied Miss Gumpert stiffly. "Perhaps you could bring the drawers of your butterfly collection downstairs and display them on the pool table instead."

"I don't mind going to his bedroom," said Katie. "I'd like to see this house. It's amazing—really fabulous."

"Very well," said Miss Gumpert. "I will accompany you on the house tour."

"I assure you, Miss Gumpert, I can find my way around this house by myself," said Brian sarcastically. Miss Gumpert nodded, tight-lipped, and retreated down a long hallway. Brian led Katie to the kitchen. The first thing she noticed was a long row of copper pots hanging from the ceiling. They were so highly polished she could see her reflection. On every windowsill there was a row of potted red geraniums.

"Want a snack, honey?" Katie looked around and saw a plump lady in a white uniform kneading dough on a marble slab. She had white hair that fell in wisps out of the bun on top of her head.

"Hi, Emma," said Brian. "Emma, this is my friend, Katie, from school. Katie, this is Emma Mae, our cook and geranium gardener. She can make a geranium flourish in the pitch dark!"

"Pleased to meet you," said Katie, extending her hand to Emma.

"Don't touch me, honey. I'm covered with flour."

Emma washed and dried her hands. "Sit yourself down for some fresh-baked apple pie," she said, cutting two slices with a knife.

"Thank you," said Katie. "I love apple pie."

"All he does is read," said Emma, shaking her head. "Brian's got too much on his mind. He needs a pretty young girl like you."

Katie blushed.

"Here, honey, eat more." Emma dropped another sliver of pie onto Brian's plate. "I've got to fatten you up 'fore your mamma gets home."

Emma patted Katie on the head. "You remind me of my youngest daughter, Letty. She got 'cepted to college, my Letty Mae. She's done real good." Emma snipped a wilted geranium flower off a stem with her fingernail.

"Hey, Emma," said Brian, chewing on his pie. He lowered his voice. "Will you get rid of The Gump? She's trying to tail me."

"Lord almighty! That woman acts like she got nothing better to do. Don't you worry, honey." She gently pinched Brian's cheek and chuckled.

Katie finished her pie and got up to wash the plate in the sink.

"Never you mind, honey," said Emma. "You go look at all them beautiful bugs." Emma winked at Brian.

"Follow me," said Brian, as they slipped out the kitchen door. "These stairs will take us into the servants' quarters. Then I'll show you the master bedrooms."

"I really like Emma Mae," said Katie, following Brian up the back kitchen stairs.

"We used to have a black cook, but I think Emma Mae's southern cooking is just as good. Emma Mae is the only person around here who has the guts to stand up to my mother."

"How many rooms do you have?" asked Katie. She felt relieved that Brian's mother was out of town.

"We've got nine master bedroom suites and three bedrooms with baths for the help," Brian answered. "Emma Mae and Miss Gumpert always stay here, but Miss Ingersoll travels with my mother. She's her personal secretary."

"What about your driver? Where does he live?"

"You mean Oscar? He and his wife live in an apartment above the garage. They have a grown-up son but he's still back in England."

Katie walked beside Brian along a baby-blue carpeted hallway.

"You could get lost in this place," she said, following Brian down the hall.

"It gets spooky sometimes at night. I'd trade this mansion for a simple cabin by a lake any day."

Brian's bedroom was three times the size of Katie's. On one side of the room there was a built-in wall unit with bookcases, a gigantic TV, VCR, and shelves and shelves of CDs and video games. One long shelf was lined with books bound in green leather. An elephant head with tusks was mounted on the wall above the bed.

"My stepfather shot that elephant in Africa. He shot it before elephants became an endangered species, not that he would have cared. It used to be in his study downstairs. After he moved out, my mom wanted to get rid of it. I felt sorry for the elephant, so I asked if we could hang it in my bedroom."

Brian pulled out a large shallow drawer full of bugs with tiny pins stuck in their backs. "We had my display cases built directly into the wall," he said. He turned on a spotlight that beamed from the ceiling onto the shelves of his collection. He handed Katie a large magnifying glass.

"This butterfly is amazing!" said Katie. She put the magnifying glass directly above the paper-thin wings. "What is it called?" she asked.

"That is an *Egybolis vaillantina*. I caught that one in Kenya."

Brian opened another large shallow drawer. There were twenty or thirty butterflies mounted underneath the glass.

"This is amazing," said Katie again.

"I've been collecting butterflies ever since we lived in France. We'd go out to our country estate on the weekends. The fields there were full of butterflies. I've collected insects for five or six years now. Look at this one." As Brian held the magnifying glass over a two-inch millipede, his arm gently touched Katie's.

After Brian showed Katie every drawer of his B and B collection, he pointed out his rare book collection. "My mother gave me a complete set of Shakespearean plays for my birthday."

What a terrible present, thought Katie. "That's nice," she said. "You must really love Shakespeare."

"He's, of course, brilliant," said Brian. "But I prefer more modern playwrights."

"Me, too." Katie quickly changed the subject. "Is this your mother?" she asked, pointing to a large silver-framed photograph of a woman sitting stiffly in a high-backed chair. She was wearing a deep-red velvet evening gown with a fur collar.

"That's Miss Lilly, all right," said Brian.

"She's amazingly beautiful."

"I suppose you could say that," Brian said in a sarcastic tone. "Would you like to see mother's bedroom?"

"Sure." Katie thought it odd that Brian never referred to his mother as mom. She peeked in Brian's bathroom and saw a Jacuzzi twice as big as Willy's wading pool. As they left the room, Katie stopped in the hallway to admire the flower prints on the wall. "These pictures look like they came from England a hundred years ago," she said.

With his hand poised on an ornate gold doorknob, Brian waited for Katie in front of his mother's bedroom door.

13

Brian slowly opened the door to his mother's bedroom. "It looks like a Laura Ashley showroom," Katie gasped. "It's gorgeous!" The bedspread and the curtains were made of a pink and purple flower print. The wallpaper, carpet, and window shades had a matching pattern of yellow, pink, and purple flowers tied with tiny white ribbons. Even the tissue box matched the design.

"That's an original Renoir," said Brian. He pointed to a painting of a lady holding a dog.

"No kidding," said Katie, studying the picture more carefully. "Does your mother like art?"

"She collects mostly modern art. This Renoir is a late nineteenth-century piece."

"Do you have any Andrew Wyeth paintings? He's my favorite artist."

"We have only one original Wyeth. I'll show it to you. It's in my mother's dressing room."

Brian opened a door across the room from the Renoir. He flipped on the lights and pointed to a picture on the wall behind his mother's dressing table. "That's the original Wyeth," he said. "I think that the lady was his wife."

"I saw that picture in a book," said Katie reverently. After gazing at the painting for a moment, she turned and looked at the clothes racks that lined every wall of the room and stretched down the middle of the floor. "This closet looks like the ladies department in Bloomingdale's," Katie said, wide-eyed.

"These racks are for evening wear," said Brian. "These racks over here are for suits. This rack is for dresses. These racks are for slacks and blouses. Well, I guess you get the idea." He turned and walked back into the bedroom.

"I've never seen so many clothes in my life," Katie said, following him. "Your mother must have more than a hundred dresses!"

"My mother tries to set a fashion example," Brian explained stiffly, as if he were talking about a stranger. "She rarely wears the same outfit more than twice. Sometimes I think making money and fixing up her hair and her nails are all she really cares about in life. She never has time to spend with me, that's for sure."

"She's very beautiful," said Katie.

"Outside she's beautiful, but. . . ."

Katie looked out the window, not sure how to respond to the hurt in Brian's voice. "I'd better start thinking about going home," she said suddenly. "What time is it?"

Brian looked at the miniature gold clock with jewels in it on his mother's bureau, next to the silver comb and brush set.

"It's 4:45. I'll call Oscar to see if he can give you a lift home." Brian pushed a button marked "Garage" on a box attached to the telephone next to his mother's bed.

"Oscar, can you do me a favor? Can you run my friend Katie home?" There was a pause. Brian laughed into the telephone. "Okay, we'll meet you down by the garage." Brian hung up the phone. "He says he'd be happy to drive you home. Do want to go in the limo or the Ferrari?"

"I'll take the limousine," said Katie, mimicking an English accent.

"Yes ma'am," Brian smiled. He flipped off the lights in his mother's dressing room, closed the door, and led the way back downstairs. "I'll show you the wine cellar and audiovisual room the next time you come," he said.

"Can I say good-bye to Emma?" asked Katie. "I really like her."

"She's a lot kinder than The Gump. That woman is a real pain in the. . . ." He let the sentence hang for effect.

"Good-bye, Emma," Katie called. Emma walked into the kitchen from the pantry. Her legs looked swollen in her tight white shoes.

"Bye, honey. You come back again and see us, you hear?"

"I'll come back," Katie assured her. "You should put your geraniums in a flower magazine. And thanks again for the yummy apple pie."

Emma beamed and nodded. Brian was waiting with a tall, white-haired man next to the four-car garage. He pushed a button on a little machine. The door to the limousine garage opened automatically.

"Katie, this is my good buddy, Oscar."

"Pleased to meet you, Miss Katie." Oscar had a dignified English accent and a strong handshake. He was wearing a well-fitted gray sports coat with a white shirt and a black bow tie. His eyes were kind. Katie could sense by the way he looked at Brian that he loved him like a son.

Brian opened the passenger door to the limousine. "Would you like a soda?" he asked, climbing into the back seat. "Or perhaps you'd prefer to watch your favorite soap opera," he added, grinning. Katie looked wide-eyed as Brian flipped the channels of a small color television set.

"You must love taking kids for rides in this car. It's unbelievable! I wish my parents could afford a car like this. I want a red convertible when I get my license."

"Most often I enjoy inviting friends, but once in London I brought a chap home from school and he never talked to me again. He just talked *about* me to anyone who would listen."

"I'd never do that to you, Brian," Katie said in a surprised voice.

"What's Miss Katie's address?" Oscar asked from the front seat.

"I live at 14 Front Street," Katie answered through the glass partition.

"What is the best route between Bella Vista and Front Street?" asked Oscar.

"I haven't the vaguest idea," said Katie. "I get lost on this side of town. If you can drive us back to G.W., I know my way home from there."

"Certainly," said Oscar, tipping the visor on his black cap.

"He must think I'm a real dope," Katie whispered to Brian. "I still get lost, and I've lived in North Kent ever since kindergarten."

"This gives us more time together," Brian said softly. He leaned back in the plush black leather seat. "Are you still going to the seventh-grade recreation night on Friday?"

"I was thinking about it," said Katie, sitting back in the seat, close to Brian.

"We could meet on the G.W. steps at seven and walk in together," suggested Brian hopefully.

Katie felt Brian's warm arm touch hers as they went around a corner. He looked so out of place, sitting there on the black leather seat in his dark glasses, punk rock T-shirt, jeans, and leather sandals.

"What does you mother think of your wardrobe?" Katie asked out of the blue.

"Why do you ask?"

"Just curious."

"As you can imagine, she is mortified by the way I dress. I've got a closet full of 'proper outfits,' none of which I wear unless she begs me." Brian looked uncomfortable. "You have beautiful hair," he said. Katie sensed that the way he dressed was a delicate topic.

"Thanks," she said. "I want to have it cut short and get a perm, but my mom won't let me."

"I like it just the way it is," said Brian. "You don't look so much like the cookie-cutter seventh-grade girl."

As the limousine passed G.W., Katie moved closer to the window and looked for someone to wave to. "Would you like to come inside and meet my mother?" she asked. The house at 14 Front Street looked embarrassingly small and uninteresting compared to Brian's estate.

"Another time," said Brian. "I feel a little nervous about meeting your parents."

"Don't be worried. My parents are really cool," Katie reassured him as she climbed out of the limo.

"I wish I could say the same about mine." Brian's voice sounded bitter. "I'll see you tomorrow in homeroom."

Katie waved as the limo pulled away from the curb.

"Hi, Tee-Tee," Willy called from the sandbox as Katie ran up the driveway.

"Hi, Willy, where's Mom?" Without waiting for an answer, Katie burst open the screen door. She dropped her book bag on the kitchen table and followed the sound of her mother's bassoon.

"Mom, you won't believe this," she said. "You simply would not believe Brian's house."

Her mother looked up and took the bassoon reed out of her mouth. "Just a second, Kate. Let me finish this phrase."

Katie tapped her foot and waited impatiently for her mother to finish playing. She began to talk excitedly as her mother laid the bassoon down on her lap. "They have originals by Renoir and Wyeth, and Brian has a Jacuzzi in his private bathroom and hundreds of CDs and butterflies and his own color TV bigger than our kitchen table. His cook

100

grows geraniums and there's a weird housekeeper and Oscar the English chauffeur. His mom is Lilly the famous wrinkle-free fashion designer—she's gorgeous and has more dresses than you and all your friends put together." Katie suddenly realized she was out of breath.

"Kate, you've had quite a day! How did you get home?"

"Oscar brought me in the black stretch limo with a TV and a refrigerator and fax machine and telephone and tissues and a reading light. I was hoping kids at G.W. would see me in the back seat."

Katie's mother laughed. "The only time I've ever driven in a car like that was when I won the Young Musicians Award in college. I got to ride from Juilliard to Lincoln Center with Leonard Bernstein. I'll never forget it."

"Mom, you just can't believe this house. It has a swimming pool and a grass tennis court and rose gardens and—"

"Where is Brian's father?"

"Oh, Brian's parents are divorced. His father lives in Hawaii and writes best-sellers. He has a stepfather, but he left, too. He used to do a lot of hunting. He didn't just hunt ducks, like Grandfather. He hunted for elephants in Africa!"

"Sounds like quite a family."

"Brian's mom is very glamorous, but I get the idea she isn't too easy to live with."

"I've seen her on a few talk shows. As I recall, she started out by making her own dress patterns and selling them from her apartment in Brooklyn. She's known to be a shrewd and rather ruthless businesswoman. She built up

101

the entire Lilly line all on her own. Now I image it must be worth a fortune."

"Mom, Brian asked me to meet him on the G.W. steps before the dance on Friday night. Do you realize that this is the first date of my life?"

"That's great, Kate," Mrs. Kelso said, looking away. "Friday will be a memorable day for us both."

Katie flipped back her hair. "That's the day you go into the hospital, isn't it, Mom?"

"Yes, at nine in the morning. Your dad and I talked to the doctor again yesterday. We have decided that if the lump is cancerous, the surgeon will operate on it immediately."

"Why don't you wait for a few days to get used to the idea?" asked Katie.

"I don't want to have to go under anesthesia twice if I can help it." Her mother sighed deeply. "I will certainly be relieved to have all this over with."

"What will they do to you, Mom?"

"Basically, we have two choices. I can either have a modified radical mastectomy or a lumpectomy."

Katie sat down in a chair. "What's the difference?" she asked.

"When you do a modified radical mastectomy, the doctor takes the breast off completely. When you do a lumpectomy, only the cancerous cells in the lump are removed, not the entire breast." Katie's mother paused for a deep breath. "After that, you have radiation treatments to be sure to catch any stray bits of cancer that might still be in your system."

"Won't you look really weird walking around with one breast?"

Her mom smiled. "You buy a falsie, kind of a rubber breast to put in your bra. You can even have surgery to make a new breast with implants."

"Which kind of operation are you going to have, Mom? I mean, if the lump turns out to be bad."

"I'm honestly not sure, Kate. I've done a lot of reading about both operations. I've also talked to another woman in the orchestra who had breast cancer over ten years ago."

"What does Dad think?"

"Your father wants me to do whatever I would feel most comfortable doing. He's been wonderful, just wonderful." Katie saw tears well up in her mother's eyes. She felt scared to see her mother look so upset.

"Do you want me to give Willy his bath?" Katie asked, trying to be especially helpful. "I don't need to start my homework until after supper."

"I'd really appreciate that, Kate." Her mother took a tissue out of the pocket of her corduroy skirt and blew her nose. "I promised to call Aunt Susan before supper. The hardest part is not knowing the diagnosis. I feel I can face anything—I just hate not knowing what it is I have to face."

Katie gave Willy his bath and made her Dad's favorite Hebrew National hot dogs for supper. After dinner, Katie put Willy to bed and told him another story about Darby the dump truck. She finished her homework and felt under her mattress for her diary. Unlocking the clasp, Katie opened the book and began to write.

Deer Dairy,

Today I was asked out by a boy for the 1st time in my life. Brain wants me to go to the danse on fri. nt. We're going to meet at 7:00 on the G.W. steps. I went to his house. It is fabulus. I loved his cook and showfur. If we had money like Brain Mom could hire a made and I'd be set free. Rite now I don't have a life of my own. Brain's mom is never home. Nither is his dad. I'd give anything to be as rich as Brain. He gets to buy any CD he wants and he owns about 1000 vibeo games. I wish the P.K.'s at G.W. had seen me riding in the limo. Mom mite have an operation on fri. She mite have a lump or the hole brest taken off. It sounds reely scary. I didn't tell Mom but I saw on T.V. that women can die of brest cansir. I hope Mom's lump is O.K. and that she duz not need an operation. Spud is going to be at the danse to. He put his arm around me at G.W. Spud is cuter than Brain but he's not as thotful.

The End

CHAPTER

14

K atie woke up at 6:05 on Friday morning, even before
the alarm clock jarred her out of sleep. She lay under
the covers and thought about her mother going to the hospital. Katie had never been to the hospital, except when
Sam hit her over the head with his toy helicopter and she
had to get four stitches. Would her mother pack a suitcase,
or did she really think she would be home that afternoon?

Katie's heart pounded quickly, the way it did when she
had to read out loud in front of the class. She decided to get
out of bed and to get dressed early. She would review her
English vocabulary words again and help her mother fix
breakfast.

"Good morning, Katie. You're up early today." Her dad
was pouring black coffee.

"Where's Mom?" asked Katie.

"Your mother is still in bed. She can't eat or drink anything this morning."

"Is that because of the operation?"

Her dad nodded. "You can't eat or drink before you have anesthesia," he said, taking the Raisin Bran off the shelf and pouring himself a bowl. "Would you like some cereal, honey?"

"I'm not too hungry, Dad. My stomach feels like a net full of Brian's butterflies."

"Have some toast," said her dad. "I know how you feel. This will be a hard day for all of us."

"When will we know about Mom?" Katie asked. "I mean, when will we know if she has cancer or not?" Katie spread butter and blueberry jam on her toast.

"We check into the hospital at 9 a.m. Your mother is scheduled to go into the operating room at eleven. They'll analyze the cells in the lump while she's still on the operating table. I imagine the surgeon will get back to me by noon."

"When will I know?" asked Katie. She tried to keep her voice from shaking.

"I'll be here when you and Sam get home from school."

"Who is going to take care of Willy?"

"One of your mother's friends from the orchestra will baby-sit for him at her house. She's got a two-year-old herself."

Katie's mother walked into the kitchen with Willy on her hip. She was wearing her favorite soft flower-print dress. Her long reddish hair was wet and smelled of herbal creme rinse. It hung down her back to dry. She slipped Willy into his high chair and put a bowl of cereal in front of him.

"Would you like me to drill you on your English vocabulary words, Kate?" Mrs. Kelso sat down at the kitchen table. She took her husband's cup of coffee in both hands and smelled it longingly, then pushed it away.

"How can you think of vocabulary words on a day like this, Mom?"

"It helps. It's good to keep my mind occupied. Hand me your book. What does preposterous mean?"

"Preposterous means contrary to nature, reason, or common sense," Katie answered.

Katie and her mother reviewed four words. They went over them twice. The second time around, Katie got three correct. Her mother added gregarious, the only word she still got wrong, to a special list of stumper words that needed another final review.

"You should do well on the test, Kate," she said. "You're pretty good with these definitions."

"Thanks, Mom. I memorized five words a day. I decided it's too hard to cram all the words into my brain on Thursday night the way Corky does."

"Can't I even have *one* sip of coffee?" Her mother closed the English vocabulary book and reached for her husband's cup.

"Not even one sip." Mr. Kelso kissed his wife on the cheek and moved his coffee cup to the other side of the table.

"Tonight's the big night, right?" he said, looking over at his daughter.

"It's nothing special, Dad, just a dance," said Katie.

Sam walked into the kitchen. He was holding a shoe box diorama of Wilbur's barnyard from *Charlotte's Web*.

"I bet you only dance with girls," he said, opening a can of dog food for Mozart.

"For your information, I'm meeting a boy on the front steps." Katie stuck her tongue out at her brother.

"Katie has a boyfriend, Katie has a boyfriend," Sam chanted.

Willy dumped his plastic cup of milk on the floor. Mozart quickly licked the spill up from under his chair.

"It certainly will be a relief to go to a nice, quiet hospital," Mrs. Kelso said, bending down to pick up Willy's cup. "What are you wearing tonight, Kate?" she asked.

"I can't decide if I should wear my white skirt and a pink blouse, or my green slacks and a purple turtleneck, or my dress with the designs from Mexico."

"I'll put your hair into a French braid. If I'm here, that is," her mother added in a low voice.

Katie felt a lump in her throat as if she were getting a choking feeling.

"I'd better go, Mom," she said, shoving the English vocabulary book in her book bag. She gave her mother a long hug. "I'll see you tonight. Good luck with your operation. I'll be thinking about you all day long."

Katie felt her mother's soft, warm breasts press against her as they hugged.

"Have a good day, love. Don't worry. I'm in good hands."

Katie grabbed her book bag and let the screen door slam behind her. She didn't even stop to say good-bye to her dad and Sam and Willy and Mozart. She was afraid that her mother might see that tears had come into her eyes.

"Don't forget what gregarious means!" her mother called behind her. "Good luck on your test."

Katie walked quickly toward school. She wanted to get to homeroom in time to review the index card of vocabulary stumpers before her test first period.

Miss Dalton was sitting at her desk correcting papers when Katie opened the classroom door. "Good morning, Katie," she said. "You look pretty this morning. Blue is a becoming color on you."

"Thanks, Miss Dalton," said Katie. She felt to make sure all the buttons on her blouse were buttoned. "I just want a chance to review my English vocabulary words one last time. Last week I didn't do so well on the test."

"Then I won't disturb you," said Miss Dalton, looking down at her papers.

Katie studied the four stumper words her mother had written on the index card. She looked at the shape of the letters in gregarious. When she looked at the word, she noticed two g's going below the line. She could think of go-go dancers on TV. She would picture go-go dancers running under a flock of birds being chased by a herd of elephants. That way she could remember that gregarious meant "pertaining to a flock or herd." Next to the word gregarious, Katie drew a picture of two go-go dancers with birds above them and elephants running behind. When she could associate a picture with a vocabulary word, she almost never got it wrong.

Brian walked into the room. He stood next to Katie's desk and looked over her shoulder. "You're a good artist," he said. "How come you made a picture of two ladies in bathing suits being chased by a herd of elephants?"

"It's too complicated to explain," said Katie. "I just like to draw."

"Are you all set for tonight? I mean, do you still want to go to the dance?"

"Not so loud," said Katie, almost in a whisper. "I'll be there, Brian, I promise. I'll meet you on the steps at seven," she said softly.

Spud bumped Brian as he pushed past him going toward his desk. "Pits is absent," he said excitedly. "Change places. Pass it on."

Katie leaned over to Meghan sitting next to her. "Spud wants us to sit in different seats in English," she said. "Cherry's absent. Pass it on."

Meghan tapped the boy next to her and whispered the message. He grinned and told Georgie.

Miss Dalton rang the brass bell on her desk. Everyone except Spud stopped talking and looked toward the front of the room.

"Please rise for the Pledge of Allegiance." Katie felt for her broken fingernail, then placed her right hand over her heart and recited the pledge. She wondered if it would hurt after the operation for her mother to pledge the flag. After attendance, Miss Dalton took out her white sheet of daily announcements.

"Dr. Ward, our principal, has asked me to remind you that tonight is our first seventh-grade recreation night. It will begin promptly at seven and end at nine. There will be faculty and parent chaperones. No smoking or alcohol will be permitted." Miss Dalton put down the announcement sheet and looked up at the class. "Dr. Ward is very strict about enforcing school rules. If any students are found smoking or drinking on school grounds, there will be very unpleasant consequences."

"Like what?" asked Elroy Flowers.

"Last year a seventh-grade girl was caught smoking in the bathroom," said Miss Dalton, clearing her throat. "She was not allowed back into school until she and her parents met with the school administration and members of the Guidance Department. It was quite unpleasant. Nothing any of you want to get involved in, I can assure you."

Katie looked around the room. Spud was tipping back in his seat with a pencil in his mouth. He was grinning and puffing on the pencil as if it were a cigarette.

"If you are interested in being on the staff of the *Golden Plume*, your writing sample is due on my desk this Monday by 3 p.m.," continued Miss Dalton. "It should be no more than one or two pages in length. Please sign your name in pencil on the back of the first sheet. Are there any questions?"

"Should it be written in ink?" asked Meghan.

"All papers submitted in the junior high should be copied over neatly in ink or typed on a word processor."

Katie glanced over at Brian. He took off his dark glasses and gave her an encouraging nod. Katie opened her assignment book and wrote down, "wright something for lit. mag. for mon." She had learned to write down every assignment, even those she thought for sure she would remember.

CHAPTER

15

When the bell rang to end homeroom, Brian waited for Katie at the door. They walked together toward the north stairwell to go to first-period English.

"I really liked your house, Brian," said Katie. "I'm glad I got to see your B and B collection."

"You made quite a hit with Emma Mae," Brian said, shifting his book bag from one shoulder to the other. "She says she's making a carrot cake on Monday in case you come back again next week."

"I love carrot cake. My mom never bakes cakes anymore. She never has time. She's always running to this meeting or to that rehearsal. Sometimes we get frozen cake from the supermarket. It's not bad." They walked into their English class.

"At least your mother comes home in between her meetings." Brian ran his fingers through his thick, curly hair. "I'll see you tonight."

"Be sure to leave all your beer and cigarettes at home," Katie said in an accent that exactly mimicked Miss Dalton.

Spud stood at the door of the English class. As each person arrived, he gave the message for girls to switch places with a girl and boys to switch places with a boy. He said to pretend to be that person all through class.

Katie traded places with a girl she didn't know from the Willard Elementary School. After a lot of coaxing, Brian traded places with Spud and sat down next to Katie in the back row. The substitute teacher sat on top of her desk. She swung her legs back and forth. Katie thought she looked more like a high school student than a real teacher. The name "Ms. Merrill" was written in perfect cursive writing on the blackboard.

"Good morning, class."

"Good morning, Ms. Merrill," the class responded politely.

"Let's begin by taking attendance. Mr. Cherry left me with a seating chart." As Ms. Merrill called each name, the person sitting in the chair said, "Present." Elroy Flowers even said "Present" with a Chinese accent when she called "Ping Dong Wee."

"We love English," said Spud. "None of us would miss English for the world."

Ms. Merrill looked down at the seating chart. "Brian, I'm so glad you like English. When I was your age, it was

113

my favorite subject. I majored in nineteenth-century literature in college."

Katie raised her hand.

"Yes, Ellen?"

"What were some of your favorite books when you were in junior high?" she asked. Katie was a master at getting a teacher off the subject. After Ms. Merrill spent twenty-three minutes discussing her favorite young-adult novels, she passed out white paper and asked the class to put on the regular heading and to number the paper from one to twenty. Katie wrote the name Ellen Ramsey at the top of her page. She glanced over at Brian's paper. She numbered her paper exactly the way he had numbered his.

"Mr. Cherry asked me to give you the weekly vocabulary test," she said. "I think you know the procedure. When you have finished the test, make sure your name is on the paper and look up at me. Then we can correct the papers together."

Katie concentrated hard on each vocabulary word. When she got to the word gregarious, the two g's below the line reminded her of the go-go dancers. Instantly, the picture of two dancing ladies being chased by a herd of elephants with a flock of birds flying above their heads came into mind. She matched gregarious, the hardest word on the list, with the definition "of or pertaining to a herd or flock." After everyone had finished the test, Ms. Merrill instructed the class to exchange papers with the person sitting to his or her left. Katie corrected Brian's paper, which had "Spud" written at the top.

Ms. Merrill stood at the front of the room holding her roll book. "Now I'd like each of you to read me your grade," she said. "As I call your name, please give me your score."

Katie looked down at her paper. She'd gotten a 95%! A swell of pride filled her chest until she realized that the name Ellen Ramsey was written in her best handwriting on the top of her page. Ms. Merrill began the roll.

"Nina."

"75%."

"Katie."

"70%."

"Elroy."

"95%."

"Brian."

"60%."

"Ellen."

"95%."

"Norman." There was a giggle from the back row. "We call him 'Spud,'" Elroy said.

"100%," Brian said grudgingly.

"Hey, great work, Norman!" Spud called from the desk assigned to Brian. He was tipping back in his chair and grinning as if he'd just won the lottery.

"I'm never doing anything that conceited dolt suggests again," Brian whispered angrily. "My whole average is ruined." He kicked the side of his desk. "Why did I ever go along with that clown's idiotic scheme?"

"I was supposed to get 95, and I got 70 instead," Katie whispered back. "I really needed that grade."

Katie looked at Spud. He was still grinning.

When the bell rang to end English class, Katie glanced up at the clock. It said 9:30. Her mother would be in the hospital by now. She took a deep breath and shoved her loose-leaf binder into her book bag.

At lunch, Katie sat down next to Corky at their usual table. Corky had a plate with four packages of saltines and a glass of water on her tray.

"Don't you feel well?" asked Katie.

"I feel fine. I'm dieting. I'm trying to lose a pound by tonight. So what are you wearing to the dance?" Corky asked, chewing on a saltine.

"Who knows? I keep changing my mind. I think I'll wear brown, or maybe blue. I'm becoming in blue."

Corky looked puzzled. "I can't decide if I should wear pants or a skirt. I think I look thinner in a skirt. What do you think?"

Katie shrugged her shoulders. "I'm worried about my mom. She is—"

"Meghan is picking me up at 6:45," Corky interrupted. "Do you want to walk over to G.W. with us?"

"No, thanks," said Katie. "I'm meeting someone on the steps. My mom is in the—"

Corky stared at her. "A boy or a girl?" she asked.

"A boy," said Katie.

"You mean to say you have a date with a boy and you didn't tell me? Katie, I've been your best friend since first grade. How could you hide this from me?"

"I'm not hiding anything, and it isn't a real date. We're just walking in together, that's all."

"So Spud finally asked you out. I don't believe it. Every seventh-grade girl will hate you for this."

"It isn't Spud. I think Spud is a drip."

"I thought you liked him!"

"Now I think he's a conceited dolp."

"You mean dolt?"

Katie nodded her head. "He's a real dolt. He's just a jock who thinks only about himself."

"So who is it? Tell me. Who's taking you out?"

"No one is taking me out. We are just walking up to the door together. That's all."

"Katie, you're driving me crazy. Is it Elroy Flowers?"

"No way."

"So, who?" Corky grabbed a saltine and put it in her mouth, forgetting to take off the plastic wrapper. "See what you're doing? You're making me lose my mind."

"Stay calm. It's only Brian. I'm meeting Brian on the front steps of G.W. at seven."

"You mean that guy Brain? The rich one who collects bugs? You're going out with him?"

"How many times do I have to tell you we are not going out?" Katie said in exasperation. "If you don't stop making such a big deal about this, I'll tell him to meet me inside the door instead."

"I'm happy for you, Katie. I really am. Brian needs a haircut and some new jeans, but otherwise he seems nice enough."

"He wrote me a poem," said Katie, looking shyly into her tomato soup. "We both like to write."

"I thought you hated to write," said Corky.

"I like to write if I don't have to spell and use good penmanship. The lady in the Learning Center says I'm creative. She says I've got intuition."

"So where is the poem? I want to see what Brian wrote you."

"It's under my mattress. I put it in my diary. He said I was intelligent and tall and slender."

"You've got all the luck. Just because I inherited fat cells from my grandmother, boys won't give me a second glance."

"You also eat a lot, Corky."

"Look at this!" Corky cried, pointing her finger at the tray. "Saltines and water, you call that a lot? I'm practically starving myself to death!"

"But you're smart and you're really friendly," Katie added loyally. "One day I'm sure a boy is going to ask you out."

"Yeah, when I'm thirty."

"Stop feeling sorry for yourself," said Katie, offering Corky a piece of her orange. "You've got lots of friends. Just because they're not in the P.K. crowd isn't the end of the world."

Corky didn't look convinced. "So tell me again what time you and Brian are meeting tonight. I'm going to go out on this date vicariously."

"Oh, no you aren't. Promise me you won't sit there and spy on us." Katie pushed her chair away from the table just as the bell rang to end the lunch period. "I'll call you when I decide what I'm wearing," she said.

Katie walked over to the table where Ping was sitting. "Are you coming to the dance tonight?" she asked.

Ping shook his head. "I go bed early for Chinese tutor school on Saturday," he said. Katie couldn't imagine anything worse than going to school on Saturday.

"We'll miss you," she said to Ping. Bambi walked by talking to Mary Ruth. "I like your hair in a ponytail," Katie called, turning her back to Ping.

"Thanks," said Bambi. "It's losing its curl from the perm I got before tennis camp."

Katie glanced up at the clock. By now the surgeon would have told her dad the news. She wished she could call her father at the hospital, but she didn't have the telephone number. Katie's mind wandered the rest of the day in school. She couldn't even figure out how to draw a three-dimensional figure in art, and art was her best subject. When the bell rang to end eighth period, Katie grabbed her book bag and walked quickly out of the room.

CHAPTER

16

Katie walked directly home after school. She didn't even stop to talk to Corky, who was chatting with Mary Ruth on the G.W. front steps. She felt too preoccupied about her mother to discuss again what she was planning to wear to the seventh-grade dance. When Katie opened the back screen door to the house, she saw her father sitting alone at the kitchen table. She noticed the deep, dark circles under his eyes. He stood up and put his arms around Katie.

"Your mother is doing beautifully," he said. "They did a lumpectomy. The surgeon feels certain that your mother has an excellent chance for a full recovery."

"You mean Mom has cancer?" said Katie, stepping away from her dad.

"The biopsy showed a small area of malignancy," her dad replied, nodding slowly. "Thanks to the mammography, it was caught in its earliest stages. Dr. Moore doesn't believe it has spread to any other vital organs."

Katie slumped onto a kitchen chair as if she'd been stunned by a heavy blow. "Can I go see her?" she asked softly. "Can I go see Mom in the hospital?"

Her father cleared his throat and tapped his right foot. "As soon as Sam gets home, I thought I'd drive you both over to the hospital. I'm not sure if they will allow you upstairs into your mother's room, but at least you can wave to her at the window."

Katie walked into the living room and sank into her father's leather chair. Mozart whimpered by her knee. She bent down and picked him up. Katie hugged the dog close to her body.

"I just can't believe this," she said to her father, feeling dazed. "Mom thought it would be nothing, just a cyst."

"It's a shock to all of us, Katie," her father agreed, tapping his right foot. "Your mother seems in remarkably good spirits, however. She's extremely thankful they discovered the cancer so early and that the operation is over and done with."

Sam walked in the kitchen door and put his skateboard on the kitchen table.

"Where's Mom?" he asked, scratching a mosquito bite.

"She's at the hospital, Sam. She had an operation this morning. They took out all the cancer. She's doing just fine."

"When's Mom coming home?" Sam asked.

"She'll be home on Monday or Tuesday. Aunt Susan and Uncle Ben are coming for the weekend with Josh and Simon."

"But it's my birthday on Sunday. Mom won't even be here for my birthday!"

"You already had your party," reminded his sister.

Mr. Kelso put his arm around Sam. "We can have our family celebration when your mother gets home from the hospital," he said.

"Can Josh sleep in my room?" asked Sam.

"Of course," said his father.

"Can I go see Mom? Does it hurt?"

"Your mother is a little groggy from the anesthesia, but she says she's not in any real pain. I thought I'd drive you and Katie over to the hospital before Mrs. Niebling brings Willy home. Children are not allowed in the hospital, but your mother says she's strong enough to stand at the window and wave."

Katie put Mozart back on the floor and followed her father and Sam to the car. When Sam volunteered to let Katie sit in the front seat by the window, she knew he must be pretty upset.

At the hospital, Mr. Kelso pulled up to the main entrance door and Katie read aloud the posted sign. "Visiting hours are from 12 to 2 p.m. and 4 to 8 p.m.," she said. In small print, the sign said, "No children under sixteen admitted without special permission." Mr. Kelso found a parking space and turned to Sam. "How old does she look?" he asked.

"About ten," said Sam, looking at his sister.

"No, seriously," said his father. "How old does Katie look?"

"I can look sixteen easily," said Katie. "Wait a minute." She reached into her purse and took out her "Passion Pink" lipstick. "Mom will kill me," she said smearing it on her lips.

"Let's see if we can't sneak you into your mother's room. She'd love to see you. Sam, I'm afraid you'll have to wait in the car. We won't be long. I'll come back down and show you where to stand to wave after Katie and I visit for a few minutes with your mother."

"Can I at least listen to the car radio?" asked Sam, climbing into the front seat. "I want my own radio station while you're gone."

"Don't blast the volume and press every button on the dashboard. I don't want to come back to a dead battery."

Katie combed her hair and put powder on her nose.

"Just look confident and keep walking," said her dad. Katie stood up straight and walked next to her father past the guard at the main entrance and the volunteer ladies in pink aprons at the front desk. They stopped in front of the elevator, and Mr. Kelso pushed the button for the fourth floor. No one said a word.

Katie looked in each room as they walked down the long corridor. Her mother's room was at the end of the hall. Ladies in blue hospital nightgowns were sitting up in long beds. Many of the patients were watching TV or chatting with a friend. A young nurse smiled at Katie as she was walking briskly down the hall.

Katie followed her dad into room 437. Her mother was lying in the bed closest to the window. Two bouquets of flowers and a large plant brightened the windowsill.

"Hi, Mom," said Katie shyly. She bent over and gave her mother a gentle kiss on the cheek. "How do you feel?"

"I feel a little woozy." Katie thought her mother looked even paler than when she'd had the flu.

Mr. Kelso sat down on the bed next to his wife. He gently took her hand. "Are you in any pain?" he asked.

"It feels uncomfortable, but there's no shooting pain. I feel like an Egyptian mummy wrapped up in all these bandages."

"Who sent you the flowers?" asked Katie.

"The roses are from your father. Grandmother Poor sent the bouquet of cut flowers, and the plant is from the members of the orchestra. It was really sweet of them to send me something. I don't even know how they knew I was in the hospital."

"The woman baby-sitting for Willy probably told them," Mr. Kelso explained. "I called her about two to see how things were going. She said Willy took a long nap after lunch. She says he's a delightful little boy."

Katie looked at her father and rolled her eyes. "If he took a long nap at noon, he'll be up late tonight."

Mrs. Kelso looked at her husband. "Who did you get to baby-sit for tonight?" she asked. Katie held her breath.

"I called the agency. They are sending a woman over at 6:30. I didn't recognize her name. I don't think she's ever sat for us before."

Katie breathed a sigh of relief. Her mother sensed her relief and smiled.

"Have you decided what you're wearing tonight, Kate?"

"I don't know yet. I think I'll wear blue."

"I'm dying to hear all the details. I'd say to call me when you get home, but I'll probably be asleep. I didn't sleep too well last night."

"Sam is waiting in the car," Dad said. "He wants to wave to you. I think I'll go down and show him where to stand to see your window. Do you feel up to getting out of bed?"

"If Kate will help me, I'll be fine."

Mr. Kelso gave his wife a kiss on the forehead. "I'll be back in a few minutes," he said. "Katie, you watch for us outside the window."

Katie sat down at the end of her mother's bed. "I felt so worried about you all day in school, I could hardly think."

"It sounds strange, but I feel blessed. Imagine if I hadn't had that mammography."

"Are you sure they got all the cancer out?" Katie asked anxiously.

"Dr. Moore feels confident that he got it all. He saw no sign that the cancer had spread. We'll get the test results about the lymph nodes in a couple of days."

"Were you really scared, Mom? Did you think you might die?"

"I never thought I'd die in the operation, but it is scary to be told you have cancer, there is no doubt about that."

"Do you promise you won't die?" asked Katie, holding back tears.

Her mother shook her head and took Katie's hand. "That is not something you can make promises about, Kate. I can only say that I have every intention of living to be ninety, just like your great-grandmother."

"When you're ninety, I'll be in my sixties. I'll take care of you."

"I'm counting on it," said her mother, giving Katie's hand a squeeze. Katie stood up and looked out the window. Sam and her father were standing in the parking lot waving at the window.

"Stand up, Mom. They're out there. I see Dad and Sam."

Mrs. Kelso sat up slowly and leaned her weight on Katie as she climbed out of bed. She waved with her left hand. Her right arm was bandaged to her chest. "The doctor says it will be a few weeks before I can practice the bassoon." She waved again and smiled at Sam.

"Good. You'll get a vacation."

"I never thought of it that way. I can lie around the house and eat candies and read novels."

"As long as you don't mind reading the novels aloud to Willy, you'll be fine!" Katie and her mother waved out the window. Sam held up a piece of paper with, "GET WELL SOON, MOM!" written in Magic Marker.

"Take good care of your brothers while I'm gone, Kate."

"Don't worry, Mom. I promise I will. I'll even make Sam eat vegetables."

Soon Mr. Kelso came back into the room and gently hugged his wife good-bye. "I'll be back by six this evening. I'll sit with you while you eat your dinner," he said.

"Have a great time at the dance, Kate. And go lightly on the lipstick!"

"What did I tell you, Dad? Mom can't be too sick if she's after me for my lipstick."

"By the way," her mother took her arm and walked slowly toward the door, "how did you do on the vocabulary test this morning?"

"I got a 95," said Katie. She decided not to tell her parents that a girl named Ellen actually got the 95.

"You're doing so well in school, Kate, I'm really proud of you."

"Thanks, Mom. Sleep well tonight. I'll call you up in the morning and tell you all about the dance."

Katie gently hugged her mother good-bye at the door of the room.

"I'll come back as soon as I get the kids settled," promised Mr. Kelso. He gave his wife another kiss and walked next to Katie down the long corridor toward the elevators.

CHAPTER

17

When Mr. Kelso drove the car up the driveway, Mrs. Niebling was sitting in the sandbox with her arm around Willy. Willy and Mrs. Niebling's son Tyler were at opposite ends of the sandbox. Willy's face was smeared with dirt, as if he had been crying. Mr. Kelso talked to Mrs. Niebling while Katie ran inside to answer the ringing telephone.

"Katie, did you decide?" Katie recognized Corky's voice.

"Did I decide what?"

"Did you decide what to wear? I'm wearing black slacks and a long-sleeved cotton pullover. The one with vertical red stripes. Mom says it makes me look thinner."

"I'm not sure. I'll surprise you," said Katie. "I can't talk now, I'm in a big rush. I've got to cook supper and wash my hair, and then iron my blouse."

"Where's your mother? How come she can't cook supper?"

"Mom's not here. Something has happened. Something serious. I'll tell you about it at the dance."

"Are your parents getting a divorce?" asked Corky.

"Certainly not! They love each other. You know that. I'll tell you at the dance." Katie hung up the phone and took three hot dogs out of the refrigerator. She put each one in a hot dog bun, poured ketchup on the top, wrapped them in a napkin, and put them in the microwave oven to cook.

"Sam, you feed Willy." Katie handed him a plate of hot dogs cut into tiny bites. "I've got to wash my hair."

"I'm off to the hospital to eat supper with your mother," Mr. Kelso said, searching for his car keys. "The baby-sitter will be here at 6:30." Usually Mr. Kelso stayed to meet the sitter before he left, but tonight Katie noticed that he was preoccupied. She gave him a quick hug as he picked up his car keys from the front hall table. "Enjoy the dance!" he called, hurrying out the front door to his car.

When Katie got out of the shower, she heard Willy screaming. She went to the top of the stairs and called to Sam. "What's wrong with Willy?"

"He banged his head. It's gotten all swollen. He tried to bite me when I put ice cubes on it."

"Did you wrap the ice cubes in a dish towel?"

"Nope."

"You were freezing the little kid's head off. Put the ice cubes in a towel and try again." Katie went into her bedroom and combed out her long chestnut-colored hair. She put her hair in giant rollers and glanced at her digital clock. It said 6:23. Katie filed her nails and fumbled under the bed for her hidden makeup collection. She held up her blue blouse to see which pink lipstick looked the best with it. Next she opened her Band-Aid box of earrings and thumbed through her collection. Choosing a pair of small clip-on earrings the shape of red hearts, she put them on her bedside table.

"Willy won't stop crying," Sam called up the stairs. "You better come down here."

The doorbell rang. "Go open the front door," called Katie. "I'll be right down." Katie threw a bathrobe on over her slip and ran down the stairs. An elderly woman in a black raincoat stood at the door.

"Is this the Kelso residence?" she asked.

"Yes. Come on in," said Sam. "Are you the baby-sitter?"

"My name is Miss Grizwald." She took off her white gloves and put them in her raincoat pocket. "Will you please hang up my coat?"

"Sure," said Sam. He took the coat and threw it over the back of a chair. "Come on in."

"I said to *hang* up my coat," the baby-sitter said. She stood still as if she wouldn't move until Sam obeyed her command.

"Sorry," said Sam, hanging the coat in the front hall closet.

"What is wrong with the baby?" asked the lady, looking concerned.

"He hit his head," said Sam. "He falls down all the time. He'll be all right in a minute."

"Come here, little boy." The baby-sitter stretched out a stiff arm in Willy's direction.

Willy ran over to Katie and flung his chubby arms around her legs.

"Let go, Willy," she pleaded. "I've got to get ready for the dance."

"Tee-Tee," he cried. Katie picked Willy up and rested him on her hip.

He threw his arms around her neck and held on tightly. "I'll take my brother upstairs while I finish getting dressed," Katie said in a hurried tone. "I'm meeting someone at seven. I'm going out on a date."

"Very well," said the baby-sitter. She changed the channel on the TV and sat down in Mr. Kelso's leather chair.

"I always watch 'Flings of Passion' on Fridays at 6:30," she announced, crossing her legs.

"But I was watching a Snoopy special," Sam protested.

"Don't you have another television in this house?"

"My mom and dad have a TV in their bedroom, but we're not allowed to watch it without permission."

"I give my permission," said Miss Grizwald, winding her watch. "Look at your program upstairs." Sam shrugged his shoulders and walked out of the room.

"Who stole the hair dryer?" Katie yelled from the top of the stairs. "It's not in the cabinet under the sink."

"I'll get it," said Sam. "I was using it to make a sawdust storm in my gerbil cage."

Katie dried her hair and took out the giant hair curlers. Her hair fell in soft curls down her back. She put on her freshly pressed, blue cotton blouse and tucked it into her white pleated skirt. "Sandals or sneakers?" she asked Willy. Willy sat on her bed sucking his thumb.

Katie took her sandals out of the closet. She glanced at the digital clock. It said 6:38. She quickly touched up her pink toenail polish and carefully fitted her wet toenails through the sandal straps. Sam stood at her bedroom door.

"I feel sick," he announced. "I think I'm going to throw up."

"When did you start feeling sick?" Katie asked.

"I started to feel dizzy when I was waiting for you and Dad at the hospital."

"Maybe you need to go to the bathroom."

"I tried. It doesn't help. I feel worse now that I've eaten supper. I feel like I'm going to puke."

Katie stepped back. "I'll get the thermometer," she said. Sam followed Katie into their parents' bathroom. Katie took the thermometer out of the medicine cabinet and shook it the way her mother always did. She put it in Sam's mouth.

"Leave it under your tongue for three minutes," she said. Sam followed Katie back into her bedroom.

"Where's my other earring?" asked Katie. "I know I put two earrings right here on my bedside table." She got on her hands and knees and felt for her earring underneath the bed.

"What's it look like?" mumbled Sam, with the thermometer in his mouth.

"It's red, and it looks like a heart," she said, showing Sam the matching earring.

"It looks like a piece of candy to me." Sam took the thermometer out of his mouth. "Those red-hot heart drops look just like that."

"We've got to leave no turn unstoned," said Katie. "I've got to find that earring."

"Don't you mean, 'leave no stone unturned'?" asked Sam.

"Put that thermometer back in your mouth," ordered Katie. "Three minutes aren't up yet."

Katie continued to look through the folds of her bedspread for her earring. "I can't go to the dance with one earring," she wailed. "It's got to be here somewhere." She stared at Willy and had a sudden, awful thought. "Oh, my God! Do you think Willy ate my earring?"

"I have a fever," announced Sam, removing the thermometer from his mouth. "I knew I was sick." He slumped down onto Katie's pillow.

"Let me see that." Katie grabbed the thermometer away from her brother. She turned the thermometer around in her fingers and tried to read the number.

"I think it says a little under 100," she said.

"See what I told you? I've got a high fever. I feel like I'm coming down with a tropical disease. It feels like malaria."

"You don't have malaria."

"How do you know?"

"Because you don't live in a tropical country, that's why," replied Katie.

"Oh, yeah? But I've got a whole lot of mosquito bites. I saw on a TV nature show that you get malaria from mosquitoes. Maybe tropical mosquitoes have migrated to the United States. I ache all over." Sam put his feet up on the bed and began to moan softly.

"Get your sneakers off my bedspread," said Katie.

The phone rang. Katie ran into her parents' bedroom.

"Hello." Katie glanced desperately at the clock. It said 6:54. "Oh, hi, Aunt Susan," she said. Aunt Susan was her mother's sister. She sounded very upset. Katie told her aunt not to be so worried. She said her mother looked the same and she had a good appetite. Aunt Susan said they would leave New Jersey early in the morning and arrive in North Kent about noon. She wanted to visit her sister in the hospital as soon as possible.

"Okay, we'll see you tomorrow," Katie said, hurrying to get off the phone. She hung up as soon as her aunt said good-bye.

Katie glanced at the clock again. It was 6:59. She rushed back into her bedroom. Sam was lying on her bed. He looked pale.

"Bring me the throw-up pot," he said weakly.

"I'll tell the baby-sitter," said Katie. "I've *got* to leave! I'm really late."

"Don't let that creature near me," groaned her brother. "I'd rather die than be touched by her."

Willy stood up and crawled off the bed. "Candy?" he said. "More candy?"

"What happens if you eat plastic?" asked Katie anxiously.

"You get sick if you eat plastic, that's what happens. But I didn't eat plastic. I've got a tropical disease. I know it."

"Not you, Sam. It's Willy. I think he swallowed my earring," Katie replied.

"Oh, my God," said Sam, sitting up quickly. "What do we do now?"

"Willy. Did you eat my earring?" asked Katie.

Willy smiled. "Candy. More candy," he said, reaching for the other earring.

"First Mom gets cancer and then I get a tropical disease and Willy gets plastic poisoning, all in one day," Sam said in a melancholy voice. "Don't go out, Katie. It's not safe."

"But I'm missing my dance!" Katie cried. "Brian is waiting for me. I promised him I'd be there at seven. I'll tell the baby-sitter. She'll know what to do."

"I'm getting into my own bed. Don't let that baby-sitter upstairs. The sight of her makes me sicker. I can take care of myself."

"Eat two aspirins," said Katie, sounding like a doctor. "You'll feel better in the morning. I'll tell the baby-sitter you went to bed early."

Katie descended the stairs as quickly as she could with Willy on her hip. When her little brother saw the baby-sitter sitting in her father's leather chair, he put his arms around Katie's neck and clung tightly.

"Excuse me, but I think my little brother might have swallowed my earring," said Katie. "I can't find it anywhere."

The baby-sitter jumped up. She rushed over to Willy and tried to pry open his mouth.

"He's already swallowed it," said Katie. "My earring looks just like those candy red-hot heart drops."

The baby-sitter tried to pull Willy out of Katie's arms.

"Come here, little boy," she said. "If we turn him upside down and slap him on the back, it might come up."

"But he's not choking. He already swallowed it. It's in his stomach by now."

The baby-sitter held out her arms. "Come to Miss Grizwald," she said in a high, sugary voice.

Willy hollered "Tee-Tee!" and buried his tear-stained face in his big sister's neck.

"I'm calling my dad," Katie announced. She carried Willy into the kitchen and picked up the telephone. She dialed the number for her mother's room in the hospital. Her mother answered the telephone.

"Hi, Mom," said Katie. "Don't worry. Everything here is just fine. Could I please speak to Dad?" Her father got on the phone.

"Dad, you better get home immediately. Sam has malaria symptoms and Willy ate my heart earring, and the baby-sitter wants to tip him upside down and hit him."

There was a pause while Katie listened to her father's voice on the phone. She nodded her head and hung up the telephone.

"My dad says he'll be here in ten minutes," she said. Willy clung to her neck. "I'll stay till my dad gets home."

Holding Willy in her arms, Katie walked over to the living room window to watch for her father's car. Suddenly she felt a strange, warm sensation by her hip. Katie looked down and saw a damp stain on her white pleated skirt.

"Willy, did you wet your pants?" she cried.

Willy nodded, nuzzling his curly red hair under her chin. Katie put her little brother down in disgust.

"I give up," she groaned, collapsing onto the living room couch.

After Mr. Kelso walked in the door, he paid the baby-sitter $5 and helped her back into her black raincoat. She put on her white gloves and left without saying good-bye.

"I'm sorry, honey," Mr. Kelso put his arms around Katie. "Thank you for staying until I got back. I never should have left the boys with a baby-sitter tonight, especially one I didn't know. I didn't want to leave your mother alone, but she seems to be doing wonderfully. Now you're late for your dance and both boys had a rotten evening."

"I'm not going!" Katie said abruptly. "I'd have to change my entire outfit and besides, I have a pounding headache."

"I feel terrible. Let me drive you over to G.W."

"I'd be too embarrassed. It's past 7:30. Brian won't be waiting for me this late." Katie felt her throat tighten. She turned her back to hide the tears flooding into her eyes.

"Aunt Susan and Uncle Ben are coming at noon tomorrow," she said quickly and rushed up the stairs.

"Are you okay, honey?" her dad called behind her.

Katie didn't answer. She slammed her bedroom door and let out a heartbreaking sob. With a box of tissues next to her on the bed, she fumbled for her diary.

Deer Dairy,

This was the werst day of my life. Mom had her
operation. She has cansir. They didn't take off the
hole brest, just the lump of bad sells. I went to the
hostible with dad. They thot I looked 16 or older so
I got to go in Mom's room. Mom looks pail. She
says that she is lucky even thow she has cansir.
Sam got a fever. He thinks its malaria or some
kind of tropical disease from maskito dites. Willy
ate my heart earing. Dad says it will come out in
his dieper. I can't beleive I missed the 7th gr.
danse. I hope Brain wont be too upset. I bet I
broke his heart. I think I'm his only freind. This was
the first date of my life and I messed it up totaly. I
could cry all nite.

The End

P.S. I know I already rote tonight but I just had the
most amazing phone call from Brain. At first he
sounded reely mad becuz he thot I didn't show up
at 7:00 on purpus. Then I told him about Mom and
her cansir. He says his mother drinks alcoehol. He
sounded reely bitter. He thinks she cares more

about her busness than about him. He said he'd
rather live in a family like mine even thow we arnt
rich. I sense he reely likes me and he is one of the
most inteligent boys at G.W. I think he dresses like
a slob to make his mother pay atention to him. He
said he mite peerse his ear before she comes
home. He says Oscer's son has a peersed ear. I
fell starving hungry.

The End

CHAPTER

18

On Saturday morning, Katie made up the guest room bed with clean sheets for Aunt Susan and Uncle Ben. Simon could sleep on the living room couch in a bedroll. Josh liked to sleep on the top bunk in Sam's room. Katie put fresh towels in the bathroom. Sam said his malaria was cured, so she made him empty all the wastebaskets on the second floor. Mozart trailed in and out of each room behind Katie. He didn't want to be left alone. Katie sensed that he knew something was different at their house.

At 11:50 a red Subaru station wagon pulled into the drive. Sam and Willy ran out the back screen door. Katie sponged off the kitchen table and followed her brothers into the backyard to greet their cousins.

"How was your trip?" Sam asked, scratching another mosquito bite.

"Dad had to drive the whole way," said Simon, climbing out of the back seat. He was a year younger than Katie, but also in the seventh grade. With blond hair and freckles, he stood shorter than Katie by several inches. "Mom gets us too lost when she drives."

"I didn't mind," Uncle Ben said, standing up and stretching his long arms. "The traffic wasn't bad. Hey, you kids look great! Where's your dad?"

"He's already gone to the hospital," said Katie. "He says for you and Aunt Susan to go over right away. I can stay here with the kids."

Aunt Susan got out of the car and straightened out her blue-jean skirt. Katie was struck by how much she looked like her mother, except for the color of her hair. Aunt Susan had more gray in her hair, even though she was the younger sister.

"Willy, you've grown so much!" Aunt Susan picked up her youngest nephew and kissed him on the cheek.

"Tee-Tee," cried Willy. He wiggled his way out of her arms and ran to Katie. He put his sticky hands around her legs and looked up shyly at his aunt.

"Where's Mozart?" asked eleven-year-old Josh, climbing out of the back seat. Sam ran inside to get Mozart. He came back leading Mozart on his leash and watched as his aunt and uncle unloaded the car. Simon and Katie helped carry in the suitcases and an apple pie in a straw basket. Josh sat on the ground holding the end of Mozart's leash, patting the dog and talking in his ear.

"He can't hear you," said Sam. "He's deaf."

"Mozart understands me," said Josh confidently. "Watch this." As Josh stood up, he said "Stand!" to Mozart. Mozart stood up stiffly and followed Josh. "See what I mean? I think he reads my lips. He loves me."

"He doesn't love you, you dip," said his big brother Simon. Josh gave Simon a dirty look. He hated it when Simon called him a dip.

"He thinks you're going to take him for a walk," continued Simon, ignoring Josh's scowl. "Naturally he gets up. You think a dog is just going to lie there when he has a chance to go for a walk?" Josh looked disappointed.

"I'm anxious to see your mom and to know she's doing all right," said Aunt Susan, climbing back into the station wagon. "I'll cook supper tonight, Kate. Your mom tells me that you like to go to the movies with your girlfriends on Saturday nights."

"Thanks, Aunt Susan," said Katie with a look of relief.

"Later, kids," Uncle Ben said, starting the car and putting it into reverse.

As the red Subaru backed down the driveway, Sam and Simon carried the last suitcase into the house.

"Can I take Mozart for a walk?" Josh asked, patting Mozart on the head. "I promise I won't let go of his leash. I've walked dogs before, when we lived in New York City, before we moved to New Jersey."

"I guess you can," said Katie. "Mom usually walks Mo before we get up. He's probably anxious to get a little exercise."

"Bye," said Josh. Mozart pulled him along the sidewalk through the red and yellow leaves that had fallen from the trees.

"So, how's your school?" Katie asked Simon when he and Sam came back outside.

"I've got a real hag for homeroom. Her name is Miss Potts, and she's got dragon breath."

"I've got good teachers except for English," said Katie. "My English teacher's name is Mr. Cherry, only we call him Mr. Pits."

"My teacher's really nice," said Sam. "She's got pointed red fingernails with silver lightning bolts painted on them."

Katie bent down to take a dirty Popsicle stick out of Willy's mouth. "He'll eat anything," she said. "Last night he ate my earring."

"Yuck!" Simon made a face.

"Where's Josh?" asked Sam.

"He took Mozart for a walk. He should be back any minute."

"You let Josh go off by himself?" groaned Simon. "We'll never see him again! He can't go around the block without getting lost."

"Mozart will bring him back," replied Sam confidently.

"No, he won't," said Katie, suddenly looking worried. "Mozart will walk for miles. He'll go on any street that has cat smells. Mozart couldn't find his way home if his life depended on it."

"You won't believe what happened to me last week," said Simon. "Me and my friend Buck and Josh went on a fishing trip to Lake Winacchi. We caught one fish before Buck tripped and hurt his ankle real bad. Then some creeps stole our bikes. Josh's dirt bike was chained to a tree so the teenagers didn't get that one. He had to ride all the way home to get help, through an awesome thunderstorm. He dodged lightning the whole trip."

"How did he find his way home?" asked Sam.

"It was amazing! He remembered every single thing he had passed on the way to the lake. He even asked complete strangers for directions. I thought for sure he'd get really confused. It's his dyslexia. I thought he'd end up in a different state."

"Tell me about it!" said Katie sarcastically. "I've got dyslexia, too, you know."

"Josh is in a special class. He's got dyslexia real bad," said Simon.

"We'd better go look for him," said Sam, looking anxiously down the street.

Katie put Willy in his stroller and gave him a box of animal crackers. "Sam, you check the streets that way." She felt for her broken fingernail and pointed to the right. "Simon, you check the streets to the left. I'll take Willy and check out the block above our house. We'll meet back here in ten minutes."

The cousins walked off quickly in their assigned directions. Willy had eaten the entire box of animal crackers by the time Katie pushed his stroller back up the drive. Simon and Sam were waiting on the back steps.

"Any luck?" she panted.

"Nope. He's gone. He's lost for sure. You had a phone call. Some guy named Brian wants you to call him."

"Give Willy more crackers," she called as she ran inside the house. Katie dialed Brian's number.

"Hello. The Straus residence, Oscar speaking."

"Hi, Oscar, this is Katie. Could I please speak to Brian?"

"Of course, Miss Katie. He's in a jolly good mood this morning."

After a pause, Brian got on the telephone.

"Hi, Katie," he said. "How's your mother feeling?"

"My dad and Aunt Susan and Uncle Ben went to the hospital to see her," panted Katie. "We've got a big problem. Josh and Mozart are missing."

"Who's Josh?"

"He's my younger cousin, and he's got dyslexia. He gets lost, and he reverses letters just like—" Katie paused, "just like some other people with dyslexia."

"How long has your cousin been missing?" Brian asked in a take-charge voice.

"A long time," said Katie, "and he doesn't know his way around town. He hasn't been here since Willy was born."

"I'll be right over," Brian said reassuringly. "You just stay calm. I'll be right there." He hung up.

"He forgot to say good-bye," said Katie to no one in particular, putting down the receiver. She walked back into the yard.

"My friend Brian is coming over," she said. "He can help us look for Josh and Mozart."

"You'd better change Willy's pants," said Sam. "He's sopping wet."

Katie carried Willy upstairs to his changing table. When she came back downstairs, a black stretch limousine was pulling up to the front curb.

"Mom's dead!" cried Sam, bursting in the back door. "A hearse is coming up our drive."

"Sam, stay calm," Katie said. "Mom's not dead. That is *not* a hearse. That's my friend Brian. He has a limo."

"Brian drives a limo?"

"Brian doesn't drive yet, you dope. Oscar drives the limo. He's the chauffeur. Come on outside and I'll introduce you."

Sam looked out the window. "Are you sure it's not a hearse?" he asked suspiciously.

"I promise you, Sam. That is not a hearse. It's Brian." Katie hoisted Willy to her hip and followed Sam out the back kitchen door. Brian jumped out of the car before Oscar had time to open the door to the back seat.

"Hi, Brian," Katie said nervously, tucking her hair behind her ears. "This is my cousin Simon, and this is my brother Sam, and this is Willy." Willy put his face into Katie's neck and peeked at Brian with one eye.

"I'm happy to meet you all," said Brian. "This is my friend, Oscar." Oscar tipped his cap. "How long ago did your cousin leave?" Brian asked in a businesslike way.

"Nice car you've got here," said Sam, scratching his leg.

"My cousin Josh took Mozart for a walk about forty-five minutes ago," reported Katie. "He started off in that direction." She pointed up the street.

"Josh has dyslexia," Simon explained. "He gets lost all the time."

"I've got an idea," said Brian. "We will systematically scan each street. We are bound to find them sooner or later."

"Can I come, too?" asked Sam.

"You had better ask your parents' permission," said Oscar.

"My parents aren't home. Katie is in charge. Can I go in the limo?" Sam looked pleadingly at Katie.

"We'll all go!" said Katie. "Only we don't have a car seat for Willy."

"We could tie him up with seat belts," suggested Sam. Oscar opened the back door and Katie hoisted Willy into the middle of the back seat. He looked like a little prince sitting with his feet out straight on the black leather seat. Katie tied two seat belts around his waist. She sat on one side of Willy and Brian sat on the other. "We'll hold him tightly," Brian assured Oscar.

Sam and Simon pulled up the folding jump seats. Sam sat down and pulled out the cordless telephone. "Can I call up my friend Aly?" he asked excitedly. "Only I can't remember his phone number." He replaced the receiver.

"Would you like an ice-cold Coke?" asked Brian.

He opened the small refrigerator under the seat and handed Sam and Simon each a can of soda.

"Do you want one, too, Katie?" Brian asked.

"If you have a straw, I'll share some ginger ale with Willy," she said.

"Can we watch TV?" asked Sam, reaching for the on/off dial of the tiny television set in front of him.

"No way," said Simon. "We've got to look out the window for Josh. Remember?"

Brian pushed a button that automatically opened the back-seat windows. "Katie and Simon, you look to the right," he said. "Sam and I will look to the left. Look up side roads, too." Oscar drove slowly up and down the neighborhood streets. Sam waved to every person they passed.

"Do you think he could have walked into town?" asked Brian.

"But that's over a mile away from our house," objected Katie.

"Mozart could be pulling Josh toward town," said Sam. "There are stray cats all over the place in town." Sam took a tissue out of the leather tissue case and pretended he needed to blow his nose.

Brian pushed another button that lowered the glass partition between the back seat and Oscar in front. "Oscar, try driving toward town," he said. "We think perhaps Josh headed for North Kent."

"Sure thing," said Oscar.

Brian stretched his arm along the top of the back seat. Katie felt his fingers touch her shoulder. She held Willy's hand tightly and didn't move a muscle.

"Maybe Josh has been kidnapped," said Simon in a worried voice. "He's really friendly when he's lost. He'll go with anyone, even a stranger."

"But no one would be dumb enough to kidnap Mozart," said Katie. "I think he's just lost. We'll find him."

"How much does this car cost?" asked Sam.

Katie kicked her brother in the leg. "You're not supposed to ask that," she whispered.

"Look," cried Simon. "I think I see Josh! He's over there by the telephone booth."

"It's him!" Sam stuck his head out the window. "Hey, Josh!" he yelled.

Oscar pulled the limo up in front of the telephone booth. Simon leapt out of the car.

"Where have you been, you dip? You had us all really worried."

"Where is Mozart?" cried Sam, scrambling out of the back seat.

"Boy, am I glad to see you!" said Josh. "I got really lost. I couldn't find your house."

"Where is Mozart?" repeated Sam.

"I tied him to a tree near a puddle so he could drink some water." Josh pointed behind the telephone booth.

Sam ran over to the tree and put his arms around Mozart. The dog was panting hard, and his back legs were trembling.

"I think he's having a heart attack," cried Sam, shaking the dog.

"Oscar knows CPR," said Brian, untying Willy from the back seat. "He can do artificial respiration if necessary."

Oscar turned off the car engine and got out of the front seat of the limousine. He walked slowly over to Mozart and bent down on one knee beside him.

Katie tried to imagine doing artificial respiration on a drooling dog. If Oscar put his mouth over Mozart's jaw, Mozart would probably be so scared he'd bite Oscar's nose off.

"That dog is plumb exhausted," said Oscar cheerfully. "He just needs a jolly long nap." He patted Mozart's head and stood back up.

"Are you okay?" Katie asked Josh.

"I'm all right," said Josh. "I called information to get your telephone number, only no one answered. Where were you?"

"We were looking for you!" said Simon angrily. "Don't you know enough not to wander off by yourself?"

"Would you like a ride home?" asked Brian, trying to break the tension.

"This car is awesome," grinned Josh, peering in the back window. "I've never been in a limo before."

"Hop in," said Oscar, holding open the door.

When Oscar pulled up to the curb at 14 Front Street, Katie saw her father and Aunt Susan and Uncle Ben sitting on the front porch. They stood up and stared in amazement as Oscar opened the car door. First Mozart jumped out, his leash trailing behind him, followed by all the children.

Katie hoisted Willy onto her hip and thanked Oscar for driving them home. "Call me tonight," she said, standing close to Brian.

He touched her hair gently. "I will," he promised.

"Thanks for helping us out, Brian," said Sam. "We may take turns getting lost. This was really fun!"

"I'll talk to you tonight," Brian repeated. "You'd better go explain what's going on to your father. He looks pretty startled."

"You want to come up and meet my dad and my aunt and uncle?" asked Katie.

"Not now." Brian suddenly lost his take-charge attitude and appeared shy. "I'll meet your parents another time when you don't have company." He gave a quick nod and stepped back toward the limousine.

"Thanks again, Oscar," called Katie as she carried Willy on her hip up the driveway. "Don't forget to call me, Brian."

"How could I forget?" Brian replied as he closed the heavy black limousine door behind him.

19

A sharp knock on the bedroom door woke Katie from a sound sleep.

"Can I hide in here?" panted Josh, bursting into her bedroom. "Sam is after me. He's got a water pistol." Josh backed into her closet, pulling the door closed behind him.

"Go away," moaned Katie. "It's Sunday. I want to sleep late." She pulled her hair over her face and lay back down on the pillow.

Sam opened the door a crack. "Have you seen Josh?" he whispered.

"No, I haven't seen Josh," Katie said crossly. "Get out of my room."

"I know he's in here," said Sam, pushing open the bedroom door. He gripped the water pistol at his waist as if it were a machine gun about to wipe out innocent bystanders.

"Get out!" demanded Katie, sitting up in bed. She held the sheet up to her neck so Sam couldn't see her nightgown with the pink lace on top.

The muffled sound of a sneeze came from inside the closet. Sam tiptoed across the room and flung open the closet door.

"I got you!" he shrieked triumphantly, pumping the trigger with all his strength. Water pulsed out in a steady spray, hitting Josh in the chest.

"Now look what you've done," cried Katie, clutching the sheet to her chin. "My closet is drenched. I'm telling Dad. You're really going to get it this time. I bet Dad grounds you for one week."

"He can't. It's my birthday!" said Sam, grinning.

Josh wrung out his T-shirt and sneezed again. "It's dusty in there," he said, wiping his nose on his sleeve.

"It serves you right. Now get out of my room, both of you." Katie fell back down on the pillow.

"Aren't you even going to wish me a happy birthday?" asked Sam as he backed toward the door.

"Go away! I'll tell you 'Happy Birthday' when I'm supposed to be awake."

Katie lay back down between the soft cotton sheets and watched the water drip from the hem of her sundress into her red bedroom slipper. The fresh smell of coffee filled the room. Katie looked at her watch. Her dad must have gotten Willy dressed. She could hear her little brother yelling "Cakes! Cakes!" from his high chair.

Josh, Simon, and Sam had finished their third batch of blueberry pancakes when Katie walked barefoot into the kitchen. The boys cleared their dishes and went into the living room to watch Sunday morning cartoons.

"I just don't understand it," Uncle Ben was saying as Katie sat down at the table. "As far as we know, there is absolutely no history of breast cancer in the family."

Katie watched her dad flipping pancakes at the stove.

"She's only forty-one and she's so full of energy," added Aunt Susan, shaking her head. Katie wondered why her aunt didn't wear makeup to hide the dark circles under her eyes.

"One in nine women will get breast cancer, according to *The Boston Globe*," her father said, handing Katie a plateful of pancakes. "Thank God we caught Rachel's at such an early stage."

Aunt Susan wiped the syrup off Willy's chin. "I've got a mammography appointment for next week," she said.

"What is a mammography anyway?" Katie asked with her mouth full.

"It's a test for breast cancer. They stretch out your breast and take an X ray of it," her aunt replied. "Once I felt a lump the size of a pea. I found it when I was examining my breasts after my period. My doctor said not to worry. She said it was only a cyst."

Katie tried to imagine self-examining her breasts. They weren't much larger than two lumps as it was.

The boys wandered back into the kitchen to get something to drink.

"Can I take Mozart for a walk?" Josh asked his dad.

Before his dad could answer, Sam offered to join him. "We can capture frogs down by the creek," he said. Uncle Ben nodded, relieved.

"Be home by noon," said Aunt Susan. "We're leaving right after lunch."

"When's noon?" asked Josh.

"You dip," groaned Simon. "Everyone knows that noon is when the sun is directly above your head."

"That kid is a moron," Simon said to Katie. "He can't remember about time or people's names or phone numbers or directions, and he thinks the month after December is September."

"He's *not* dumb!" Katie said defensively. "He just thinks a little differently, that's all. He's just got dyslexia. It's not the end of the world."

The phone rang. Katie jumped up from the table. "Hello," she said, hoping to hear Brian's voice. "Oh, Corky. It's you. How was the dance?" Katie watched as her dad began to rinse the dishes. "I wasn't there because Mom was in the hospital and Sam had a fever and Willy ate my heart earring."

"What's the matter with your mom?" asked Corky. "You said you'd tell me at the dance. I couldn't call yesterday because I was forced to go visit my grandmother."

"Mom has. . . ." Katie took a deep breath. "Mom has breast cancer." There was a long pause.

"You're kidding! Breast cancer? Does that mean she might die?"

"The doctor says she'll be cured once she gets radiated."

"When's she coming home from the hospital?"

"Tomorrow. Aunt Susan and Uncle Ben and Josh and Simon are here for the weekend. Josh got lost walking

Mozart, and Brian, you know 'Brain,' he helped us find him."

"Brian never did come to the dance. He just sat on the front steps looking pathetic."

"He called me on Friday night. At first he was furious. He thought I stood him up. Then I told him about my mom."

"You said the word breast to a boy?"

"Of course I said the word breast. What else was I supposed to say, chest cancer?"

"Spud asked where you were about ten times," Corky reported.

"No kidding! What did he say?"

"He just kept asking what time you were coming. He asked if you had a date. I think he likes you. I mean *really* likes you."

"Did he have a date?" Katie asked.

"No, but girls trailed him the whole time. He danced with all the P.K.'s, especially Bebe Hollingsworth. She got her ears pierced."

Willy stood up in his high chair and cried, "Out, out!"

"I'll get him," said Aunt Susan. She was wearing the same blue-jean skirt that she had worn on the trip up from New Jersey.

"Tee-Tee," cried Willy, refusing to be picked up by his aunt.

"I've got to go, Corky. I'll call you tonight." She lifted Willy out of the high chair and sat him in her Dad's leather chair in the living room to watch cartoons.

"I'm going upstairs to start my homework," Katie called into the kitchen.

Sitting at her desk, Katie put Butterscotch on her lap and took out her assignment pad. She'd finished her math in study hall. Under her English assignment, it said: "wright something for lit. mag. for mon." She'd made a sketch of the *Golden Plume* magazine at the bottom of the assignment book page.

Katie looked through a pile of papers on her desk for her father's college literary magazine. She found it lying under her copy of *Teen Love* magazine. The first paragraph of her dad's essay on "The Examination of Metacognition" was boring. Katie skipped to the last paragraph. Her tutor once told her that if something is well written, you can learn a lot just by reading the first and last paragraphs. Even her dad's last paragraph was boring.

Katie flipped through the rest of her dad's magazine. *If I submitted one of these stories,* she thought, *no one would ever know the difference. These people aren't famous writers. They might even be dead by now.* Katie looked for a poem or a short essay. The shortest piece was only one page long. It was about the beauty of fall foliage in Maine. *I could change the name Maine to Florida,* Katie thought. *I once went to visit Grandmother Poor in Florida in the fall.* She took out a piece of white notebook paper from her binder and began to copy the essay word for word in her best handwriting.

"Katie, telephone!" her father's voice called up the stairs. Putting Butterscotch on the floor, Katie jumped up from her desk and ran barefoot into her parents' bedroom to get the phone.

"Hello," she said.

"What's up, dude?" Katie recognized Spud's voice and held her breath in disbelief. "How come you didn't show up at the G.W. dance on Friday night?"

"I was sick. I mean, my brother was sick. He had a high fever. It looked for a while like it might be something serious—like malaria."

"Too bad. You missed a cool food fight. You want to study English together?"

"You mean study for the vocabulary chapter test?"

"Yeah. I hear the Pit gives mean review tests. Why do I have to memorize sixty completely useless words? It's not like I'm going to use the word gregarious when I hang out with the guys on the football team."

"I know what you mean," said Katie.

"Meet me fourth period after lunch in the library. Go to stack five, in the back. It's private there."

"I'll think about it," said Katie.

"I'll see you tomorrow, stack five. I'll teach you some words you'll never forget!"

"Bye," said Katie.

"So long, sweetie pie!" said Spud.

Katie went back to her room, lay on her back across her bed, and stared at the ceiling. She could feel her heart pounding. Bambi had told Corky that kids go to stack five to make out. Why would Spud want to study with her, one of the worst students in seventh-grade English? He probably just wanted to French kiss. Katie imagined Spud's tan arms gripping her tightly around her waist. She'd never kissed a boy before, except for little Willy.

Katie's daydream was interrupted by a bark. Mozart had Butterscotch trapped in a corner. The dog's ears were straight up, and he was growling. Katie could see that Butterscotch's teeth were chattering.

"Out, Mozart," she yelled, dragging the dog by his collar out the bedroom door. She walked to the corner where Butterscotch still huddled. "Poor baby," she cooed, cuddling the gerbil in her arms. "Did big Mo scare you?"

Katie put Butterscotch back into her cage. She turned up the radio's volume on the all-rock, all-the-time music station and sat down in her desk chair to finish copying the essay about fall foliage. It had colorful, descriptive adjectives in every sentence. She knew Miss Dalton would be impressed.

After lunch, Uncle Ben began to pack up the car. Sam gave Josh a shoe box to make into a habitat for his new pet frog. He filled the box with grass and dirt. Josh poked holes in the top with a fork.

Katie helped her cousins carry out the suitcases. Mozart jumped into the back seat. "Don't worry, we won't need to put him on a leash," said Sam. "He won't move. Whenever we go on a trip, he just sits in the back seat. He's real afraid we'll leave without him. The only way to get him out of the car is to dangle American cheese in front of his nose. He'll follow cheese anywhere."

"Can we take Mozart home?" Josh asked his mother.

"No, love. Mozart lives here with Katie, Sam, and Willy. But we'll come back soon and visit again."

"Can I go to the hostible to say good-bye to Aunt Rachel?" Josh asked, trying to pull Mozart out of the back seat.

"Remember, little kids can't go in the hospital," said Katie. "Only if you look sixteen, the way I do."

Aunt Susan kissed her niece and nephews good-bye. Katie had never seen Uncle Ben give her father such a long hug. Her dad put his arms around Aunt Susan. "Thanks for coming," he said. "It meant a great deal to Rachel and to the kids to have you here."

Aunt Susan looked as if she was about to cry. She put on her dark glasses and climbed into the front seat next to her husband.

"Hop in, dip," Simon called.

"I'm *not* a dip!" Josh protested as he climbed into the back seat next to his brother.

"I'll call tomorrow after Rachel gets home from the hospital," Aunt Susan said. "Don't forget to take the lasagna out of the freezer for supper."

Katie waved good-bye to her cousins and then raced back inside the house. She could hear the telephone ringing in the kitchen. She held the receiver to her ear and heard Brian's deep, slow voice.

"I called to see how your mother is feeling," he said.

"She's much, much better. Aunt Susan says her cheeks are getting pinker. She's coming home tomorrow."

"That's a relief," he said.

"Mom will have to rest a lot. Dad says he doesn't think she can pick up Willy for a while. Any word on when your mother is coming home?"

"Not for at least another month," Brian said in a discouraged voice. "She's flying directly to the Orient to buy fabric after she finishes with the fashion shows in Paris."

"It must be lonely in your house, especially since you don't have any brothers and sisters."

"Luckily, I have Oscar and his wife and Emma Mae, not to mention The Gump. We make a rather eccentric family."

Katie remembered that eccentric was one of the vocabulary words on the review test.

"Are you planning to submit anything for the lit club?" asked Brian.

"I'm writing a piece about the flickering fires of autumn," said Katie.

"I'm submitting an allegorical essay. I also wrote several poems over the weekend. I wasn't planning on showing them to anyone, except perhaps to you."

"Gee, Brian. I'd be honored."

"What period do you have off for lunch tomorrow?" Brian asked.

"I'm off fourth period."

"Meet me in the library. I'll let you read what I wrote."

"The library?" Katie swallowed hard, remembering Spud's call. "How about meeting after school instead?"

"I'm meeting with Dr. Ward tomorrow after school. It's something about a problem-solving convocation on systems thinking. It's part of the gifted and talented program. Let's rendezvous at lunch."

"All right," said Katie hesitantly. "I'll see you tomorrow." Katie hung up the phone. She went into her bedroom, took her diary out from under the mattress, and worked the combination.

Setp. 20

Deer Dairy,

Unkle Ben and Ant Susan went back home to N.J.
Simon is reely mean to Josh. He calls him dip and
dieper face and he makes fun of his dislexia. Mom
is doing great. Dr. More says she can come home
tomorow. I think Ant Susan is reely upset. Heredity
is important in brest cansir. I'm going to learn how
to feel my brests every month just in case. Spud
wants to make out 4th period in the lib. stacks.
He's cute but he's also conseeded. Maybe he puts
kids down because he's got dislexia too. Brian
wants to meet me 4th period to show me his
pomes. I'm reely confused about what I should do. I
wish I could talk to Mom. Brian wants me to try
out for the lit. magazeen. I copied a story from
Dad's lit. mag. Miss Daltin wood never except me
if she saw how I spell. Its the only way I can rise up
from being a Dork for the rest of my life. Besides
being on a lit. mag. reely impresses colloges. I wish
I could wright like Brain.

The End

CHAPTER

20

Katie woke up on Monday morning dripping with perspiration. In her nightmare, she had been handcuffed to a police officer in the principal's office. Miss Dalton had accused her of plagiarism after an anonymous tip that "The Fiery Flames of Autumn" was not her original writing. After Katie pleaded for forgiveness, the principal demanded that she copy every word in the dictionary three times. He estimated it would take her six years.

Katie took a tissue out of the box on her bedside table and wiped the sweat off her neck. Her heart was still racing. It was 6:35, ten minutes before the alarm would ring. Climbing out of bed, Katie decided to take a shower. Usually she didn't wash her hair on Monday mornings, but today was a special Monday. Her mother was coming home from the hospital. Her heart raced even faster when she remembered about Brian and Spud and fourth period in the stacks.

At breakfast, Katie pushed the bowl of cereal away from her place at the table. "I'm too nervous to eat," she said.

"Try a piece of toast," her father suggested. "You should have something in your stomach."

"Dad, I've decided to submit some creative writing to be on the literary magazine, just like you did when you were in college."

"That's great, Katie. Do you want me to proofread what you wrote?"

Katie paused and looked at the soggy cornflakes in the cereal bowl. "No thanks, Dad. I looked up all the hard words in the dictionary myself. I just wrote a short piece about autumn in Florida."

"Sounds interesting," her father said, handing her a piece of toast with strawberry jam on top.

"I'll eat this on the way to G.W." Katie flung her book bag up over her shoulder. "I want to get to school early to talk to Corky. I didn't see her all weekend."

"Your mother should be home by the time you and Sam get back from school. Remember, she won't be quite as chipper as usual," her father warned.

"I don't care if she sleeps all day long. I just want Mom home again."

Katie gave her dad a quick hug. "Have a good day, sweetheart," he called as she ran down the drive, holding the piece of toast in one hand and her book bag in the other. Still feeling too nervous to eat, she threw the toast into the bushes at the end of the drive and walked quickly through the damp grass to school.

In homeroom, Miss Dalton read the daily announcements. "I'd like to remind you all that the submissions for the *Golden Plume* literary staff are due on my desk by three this afternoon," she said. "How many of you plan to try out for the literary staff?"

Brian, Stephanie, Bambi, Nina, and a new boy named Andy raised their hands. Brian gave Katie an encouraging nod. Katie slowly raised her hand, too.

"Great. I'm happy to see so many people interested in this club. Having been the faculty advisor for four years, I can assure you that it is both a pleasure and a privilege to be chosen as part of the editorial board. I wish you all good luck."

Spud snickered. Katie could hear him whisper something about "eggheads" to the kid sitting next to him.

After the bell rang, Spud picked up Katie's book bag. "I'll walk you to first period," he said. He put his arm around Katie's shoulder. "How come you want to be in that stupid club?" he whispered close to her ear. "You can't write. You go to the Learning Center."

"I like to write," said Katie, "even if I don't spell perfectly." Katie felt Spud's warm hand on her bare shoulder.

"I bet you just want to be with that stuck-up egghead. He thinks he's so superior, just because he's in advanced classes."

"Brian's a good kid," said Katie, "even if he is smart." She pulled away from Spud's arm.

"Don't forget, sweetie pie. I'll see you after lunch in the stacks." Spud winked at Katie and sat down at his desk in the back row of Mr. Cherry's English class.

"Good morning, class," said Mr. Cherry, scratching his beard. "This morning, I'd like to have individual conferences regarding the creative writing assignment you handed in last Thursday. You have a choice this period of studying for your unit vocabulary test on Wednesday or beginning your homework assignment in the anthology book."

Katie took out her anthology and turned to page 146. At least they didn't have to read the story out loud. When she read out loud, her eyes skipped words and repeated lines. After Mr. Cherry talked to Meghan, he asked Katie to come up to his desk.

"This is a fine piece of creative writing, young lady." Katie looked over her shoulder to make sure Mr. Cherry wasn't still talking to Meghan.

"You have keen powers of observation and an eye for detail. Your narrative voice is fresh and even flowing. Do you write often?"

"Well, actually, I write in my diary every night," Katie answered nervously. "I also like to write letters. When I write letters or in my diary, I don't have to worry about spelling. I just write words the way they sound."

"Unfortunately, Miss Kelso, the English language does not always make phonetic sense. Your spelling is definitely a weak skill area, but then I understand from the guidance counselor that you have dyslexia." Mr. Cherry cleared his throat. "If you proofread more carefully, you might catch mistakes like writing 'gril' for 'girl,' as you did here in the first sentence."

"Usually my mom helps me proofread, but she's in the hospital."

"I'm sorry to hear that. I hope she has a swift recovery," said Mr. Cherry. "Perhaps if you write more consistently on the word processor, using a spell-check program, you can greatly improve the technical quality of your work. From a creative, literary point of view, you write very well."

"Gee, thanks, Mr. Cherry." Katie looked at him in amazement.

"This paper would have been an 'A,'" said Mr. Cherry, "except for all the spelling and punctuation errors." A large "B" was written at the top of the page in red ink. "I look forward to your next short story," said Mr. Cherry.

Katie sat down and tried to concentrate on reading page 147 in her English anthology. The image of being handcuffed to the police officer in the principal's office kept running through her brain.

At the end of third period, Katie maneuvered her thin body through the rows of desks. She wanted to be one of the first in line at the cafeteria. Corky had already saved her a place at a table. She was munching on a bulging bologna sandwich with a mound of potato chips beside it.

"Hi, Katie," cried Corky, with her mouth full. "How's your mother doing?"

"She's coming home from the hospital today," said Katie. "What do you recommend for lunch?"

"Avoid the mystery-meat sandwich," Corky warned.

"Actually, I don't feel like eating anything for lunch today."

"Are you sick?"

"No, but my stomach feels like a washing machine churning around problems. I've got a lot on my mind."

"What's wrong?" Corky stopped chewing and looked at Katie.

Katie lowered her voice. "There is something I have to tell you," she whispered.

"What is it? What's wrong?" asked Corky. "Did you fail your English paper?"

"Nothing like that. It has to do with boys."

"Boys?"

"You won't believe this, but—"

"Mind if I join you?" Brian stood next to Katie's chair, holding his lunch tray.

"Sure. Take the load off your feet," said Corky. "Katie was just about to tell me some important news about boys." Katie kicked Corky under the table. Corky winced as she chewed a large mouthful of potato chips.

Brian blushed and pretended he didn't hear. "Did you hand in your writing sample for the lit magazine?" he asked Katie, sitting down and taking a bite of his tuna fish sandwich.

"Not yet. I'm going to turn it in after next period. I may still make some minor revisions."

"After lunch, let's go up to the library. I want to read you the poems I wrote over the weekend. I can't stand the racket in this lunchroom."

Brian took a bite of potato salad and then turned his head suddenly. He stretched his neck to look over his shoulder at his back.

"What's wrong?" asked Corky.

"It looks like you're bleeding!" cried Katie. "I think you've been shot!" Katie jumped up and pressed her napkin against the red, sticky mess on Brian's T-shirt. Something oozed in globs from under the napkin.

"Bull's-eye!" came a victorious cry over the voices in the lunchroom. Spud took a long plastic straw out of his mouth and folded his arms triumphantly over his chest. The ketchup bottle was the only thing on the plastic tray in front of him.

"I saw that," cried Mr. Cherry as he strode toward Spud from the faculty table. "Please follow me, young man, without discussion."

Spud stood up, smiling broadly. "See you later, sweetie pie," he called to Katie.

"Look, your shirt is ruined!" cried Corky. "It's covered with ketchup."

"You can't wear this, Brian," said Katie. "You'll have to change into something else." She glanced disgustedly at Spud's broad back as he followed Mr. Cherry out of the cafeteria.

"I could mutilate that kid," said Brian between clenched teeth. "If I were not so opposed to physical brutality, he'd be pulverized."

"He was just kidding around," said Corky. "He didn't mean to really hurt you."

"He embarrassed me in front of my friends. That is more hurtful than any physical pain."

"I bet you could find a clean shirt in the lost and found," said Katie, trying to be helpful.

Without another word, Brian stood up from the table.

"Can I eat the rest of your potato salad?" called Corky.

Brian continued to walk through the door without turning around. Georgie yelled out, "Brian doesn't need food. He's got enough brain power to last a lifetime."

"Go ahead and eat it," said Katie, sitting back down. "I bet Brian's not hungry anymore. That Spud can be a real creep."

"Yes, but he's such a doll," said Corky, taking a large mouthful of potato salad. "Aren't you eating anything? Here, take this." Corky put a piece of her sandwich in front of Katie. "If you crush potato chips on top, it makes it really great."

"I'm really not hungry. I've got a headache." Katie pushed her chair away from the table. "I'm going to work on my writing sample for the literary magazine. I'm handing it in next period."

"Want me to proofread your spelling?" asked Corky.

"Thanks, but no thanks." Katie stood up and pushed in her chair.

"Wait a minute. You didn't tell me your problem about boys."

"I'll tell you later. I'll call you when I get home from school. I haven't got much time. Right now I've got something more important to do."

"What's more important than talking about boys?"

"Honesty, for one thing," said Katie under her breath.

Corky shook her head and took a long sip of chocolate milk.

Katie hurried out of the cafeteria and down the hall to the empty art classroom. She felt relieved that Spud had been marched off to the principal's office by Cherry-Berry. Now she didn't have to decide if she would let him French kiss her. She went into the room, closed the door behind her, and sat down at a table. Then she unzipped her book bag and took out her loose-leaf notebook. The story about the "Fiery Flames of Autumn" was neatly tucked into a pocket in the front of the notebook. Katie took out a fresh piece of white theme paper and a dull pencil. She dropped her book bag under the art stool and began to write.

Deer Miss Daltin,

All my life I've loved to wright. I wright in my dairy every night. Once in 4th grade I even began a noval. Sinse first grade, I've had dislexia only at first it wasn't dieagnosed. I had to go to the Resorse Room in elementaery sckool. Now I'm in regular classes at G.W. but I go for help in the Learning Center and I have my tutor named Mrs. Finch. Lots of kids think I'm stupid just because I have a learning difrence. They don't know I'm a good thinker and I can solve pratical problems like when I babysit for my little brothers. Mr. Cherry even said I'm a good story wrighter with a naturally fresh voise.

I'm getting sick and tired of seeing kids get teezed because they read too slowly or read too well or speek Chineeze or overeat like my best freind Corky. I want to be on the Staff of The Golden Plum Mag. because I have a good imajination and I love to draw and to wright stories. I want to prove to kids that just because you are a little diferent, that doesn't mean you are weerd. My Mom and my Ant Susan both have dislexia too. My Mom is in the Boston orkestra and Ant Susan works with computers in a bank. I plan to be a writer or an artist or a peediatrision when I grow up.

If you except me onto the Golden Plum Lit. Staff, I promise I'll work hard. I won't let you down.

P.S. I'm probly the worst speller in 7th grade.

Katie wrote her name lightly in pencil on the back of the page. She put the white sheet of paper in the pocket of her loose-leaf notebook on top of "The Fiery Flames of Autumn," and she hurried down the hall as the bell rang for her fifth-period class.

Miss Dalton was sitting at her desk when Katie knocked on the classroom door.

"Excuse me, Miss Dalton. I want to submit my writing sample for the Literary Club."

"You're just in time, Katie," said Miss Dalton, smiling. "We're meeting this afternoon to choose the new staff."

"Actually, I have two pieces. One is a story that I recopied neatly in ink and the other is more like a letter. I'm afraid it's written in pencil."

"We've got a great many submissions to read, so I'd rather you submit only one. Which piece do you feel reflects your best writing?"

Katie held "The Fiery Flames of Autumn" in one hand and her letter to Miss Dalton in the other. She glanced from one hand to the other. "This one," she said, putting a page quickly on the desk.

"Thank you, dear. The staff will review all the submissions this afternoon. We'll announce the new literary board tomorrow in homeroom."

In the crowded hall, Katie spotted Brian wearing a G.W. football team sweatshirt. The sleeves hung down below his hands. Seeing his grim face, Katie suppressed a smile.

"I found this in the lost and found," said Brian. "I feel like an idiot in this thing."

"Better than going around looking like you've been stabbed in the back," said Katie.

"In a manner of speaking, I *was* stabbed in the back. In every school I've attended I've been tormented by kids like that 'Spud the Stud.' One day, I'll learn how to simply ignore morons like him."

173

"Brian, I've got to talk to you. Can we wait to read your poems later? There is something I have to tell you."

"Is something wrong?"

"Not exactly." Katie looked at the floor. "I just wanted to tell you I submitted my writing sample to Miss Dalton."

Brian led Katie into an empty chemistry classroom and closed the door. "Great! I'm sure you'll get nominated," he said confidently.

Katie shook her head and put her book bag down between her legs. "You don't understand," she said, flipping her hair over her shoulder. "You see, I told Miss Dalton about my learning difference. I told Miss Dalton I have dyslexia."

"You have dyslexia?" Brian's voice cracked. "You seem like such a good student!"

"I love to write, but I read really slowly, and my spelling is terrible. I'm like Josh. I get lost all the time, and I still mix up Corky's telephone number and the combination to my locker."

"Did you know that Robin Williams and Cher have dyslexia?" said Brian. "I read all about dyslexia in *Time* magazine."

"It's very common. Millions of people have it," said Katie. "My tutor said there are lots and lots of famous dyslexics, like Greg Louganis and General George Patton and Hans Christian Andersen."

"I knew immediately you'd be a good writer."

"How on earth did you know that?" asked Katie, looking surprised.

"Because of your empathy," Brian continued. "You seem to get into people's heads and understand their feelings. I trusted you the first time I talked to you. I don't usually feel that way about kids my age."

"I never thought of it that way," said Katie. "Lots of times kids talk to me about their problems. I really feel emotions. Even TV commercials make me cry, like the one of the bride putting on baby powder before her wedding."

"When you can get inside your character's head, it makes for good writing," Brian continued.

"Even so, I'll never get accepted onto the literary staff," said Katie. "The piece I submitted was written in pencil. I'm sure it had lots of spelling mistakes. I didn't even have a chance to proofread it or to make a second draft."

"We'll see," said Brian, picking up her book bag and opening the classroom door. "You want to come over to my house this afternoon? Emma Mae baked your mother a chocolate layer cake."

"That's really sweet of her," said Katie, following Brian out of the chemistry lab. "But I'd better go straight home today. Mom's coming back from the hospital. I can't wait to see her."

"I'll call you tonight," said Brian. "Maybe I can read my poems to you over the telephone."

"Call me any time," said Katie, smiling. She watched as Brian took long, awkward strides down the hall to his advanced math class. He rolled up the sleeves of his G.W. football sweatshirt and gave a quick wave in her direction.

21

It was strange to see the shades in the front bedroom pulled down during the day. Usually there was light and fresh air in every room of the house. Katie walked slowly up the driveway. Her legs ached, and she had a throbbing headache just above her eyes. Her dad's car was parked in the driveway. Katie noticed a wilted red flower lying on the front seat.

She pushed open the back screen door and called out, "Mom, are you home?"

"Not so loud, Katie," her dad's voice warned from the living room. "Your mom and Willy are both taking a nap."

"How's Mom feel?" asked Katie, dumping her book bag on the couch.

"She's thrilled to get back to her own bed, but even the trip home from the hospital exhausted her."

Katie heard Sam opening the back screen door. He ran into the living room followed by Mozart. Sam looked around the living room. "This place looks like the funeral room when Grandpa Poor died. How come we got so many flowers?"

"People sent these flowers to your mother in the hospital." Mr. Kelso picked a dead carnation out of a bouquet and dropped it in the wastebasket.

"How come they don't send candy instead, or something useful?"

"Your mother said to tell you to go upstairs the minute you both got home. She's extremely anxious to see you."

Sam raced up the stairs, followed by Katie and Mozart.

"Don't wake up Willy," called Mr. Kelso behind them.

Sam opened his parents' bedroom door a crack. It was dark inside the room with the shades pulled.

"Mom, are you awake?" he asked, tiptoeing toward the bed.

"Sammy, love, come here and give your mother a hug."

Sam stood by the side of the bed. "Can I touch you?" he asked. "Doesn't it hurt to hug?"

"It never hurts to hug my children. Come here, both of you. I've really missed you." Their mother held out her arms.

"We missed you, too, Mom." Katie smelled the herbal creme rinse on her mother's clean hair.

"Especially Willy. He was a real pain while you were gone," said Sam.

"Poor baby. He had no idea where I'd disappeared to. But now I'm home and safe, and all I have to do is get my strength back." Katie thought her mother looked beautiful even without makeup.

"You don't have to go to the hospital ever again?" asked Sam.

"Only to have radiation treatments. They'll start in a couple of weeks."

"Ma-ma, Ma-ma," came a wail from Willy's room.

"Oh no! We woke up Willy. Kate, be a love and go change his diapers."

"Sure, Mom," said Katie.

"Mozart wants to get up on the bed," said Sam. "He keeps pawing at the bedspread and trying to jump up."

"Your dad will kill me, but put him on the bed."

Sam lifted the dog up onto the double bed. Mozart panted excitedly and licked Mrs. Kelso in the face. He walked around in a circle two times and sat down directly on her lap.

"Move over, Mo," she winced. "Sit beside me, not on top of me!"

"He can't hear you, Mom," said Sam, pushing Mozart onto his father's pillow.

Willy ran into the room in his best red overalls. "Ma-Ma," he called. He tried to climb up onto the bed. Katie gave him a gentle push from behind. Willy crawled onto his mother's lap and put his arms around her neck.

"Doesn't that hurt?" asked Katie. "Do you want me to take him off the bed?"

"No, leave him up here. I missed you all so much!"

"This is a cozy scene," said Mr. Kelso, smiling as he walked into the bedroom. "Who allowed Mozart up on our bed—on *my* pillow?"

"He's allowed on our bed once a year, dear. Today is the day! So tell me what happened while I was in the hospital."

"I got an 'A' on my diorama project about Wilbur and I kicked a goal in soccer," said Sam, climbing onto the bed. "Josh and Simon were real fun, only Josh and Mozart got lost. I got a fever when you were gone, but Katie took care of me."

"Katie has really been an enormous help," added Mr. Kelso. "I don't know how I could have managed things without her."

"Mom, you're home just in time to drill me on sixty vocabulary words for the review test. Mr. Cherry said I was a pretty good writer. He even gave me a 'B' on my first short story."

"Katie has decided to try out for the G.W. literary magazine, just like her old dad," said Mr. Kelso proudly.

"Don't get your hopes up. I'm never going to be accepted," said Katie, rubbing the pain in her head above her eye. "I told Miss Dalton about my learning difference. I didn't even copy over what I wrote."

"I thought you wrote a theme about autumn in Florida," her father said.

"I changed my mind. I threw that one away."

Mozart stood up and walked around in a circle.

"Katie, take him out. Quick!" warned Sam, "before there is an accident on Dad's pillow."

"Katie's done more than her share, Sam. *You* take him out. The leash is hanging by the back door." Sam lifted Mozart off the bed and followed him down the stairs.

"Let's order pizza tonight," suggested Katie. "I'm weak from starvation."

"Pizza it is," agreed her father. "We'll have an early supper so your mother can get some sleep. I'll drill you on the vocabulary words myself tonight."

The phone began to ring and Mrs. Kelso picked it up. "It's for you, Katie. It's a boy," she added, her hand over the receiver.

"I'll get the phone downstairs." Katie hopped off the bed and ran down the stairs to the kitchen telephone.

"Hello."

"Katie, this is Brian. Was that your mother who answered the telephone?"

"That was my mom, all right. She's home in bed."

"I hope I didn't disturb her."

"She wasn't sleeping. We were all just sitting on my parents' bed talking. Even Mozart got up on the bed. Maybe one day you could come over for supper and meet my Mom and Dad."

"I'd really like that." There was a long pause. "Actually, I called to see if you're free on Saturday night. The Grateful Dead is giving a concert in the Boston Arena."

"You mean, you're asking me to a rock concert?"

"Would you rather go to a symphony or maybe a play? I could arrange that, too," he said quickly. "Tell your parents that Oscar will drive us into the city and back home again. That is, if you want to come."

"What, are you kidding? I adore the Grateful Dead. I hear their music on the radio all the time. I'll have to get permission. I'll call you back." Katie tried to keep her voice from trembling.

"By the way, Oscar is going to drop off a plant and Emma Mae's cake around five tonight. He's taking the limo out to pick up lobsters for supper."

"Thanks, Brian," Katie said. "We're having pizza. Yum—pizza and chocolate layer cake. It's my absolute favorite meal. I'll call you later."

Katie hung up the phone and dialed Corky's number. "Corky. You won't believe this!" Katie panted into the telephone. "Brian asked me to a Dead concert. He wants me to go into the city with him on Saturday night!"

"Oh, my God!" gasped Corky. "Did your parents say you could go?"

"I haven't asked them yet. He just called me. You are the first person to know."

"My mother would croak. She probably won't allow me to go to a rock concert until I'm a senior. What are you going to wear?"

"How do I know? First I've got to talk to my parents. I'll call you back." Katie hung up the telephone and raced up the stairs to her parents' bedroom.

"My friend Brian just called," Katie told her mother excitedly. "He's the kid who helped find Josh when he and Mozart got lost. He says his chauffeur is about to bring us a plant and a chocolate layer cake that Emma Mae baked. I bet it's a geranium plant that Emma Mae raised in her kitchen."

"That's so sweet of her. I deserve a thick slice of chocolate cake! The hospital food was terribly dull."

"Mom, Dad, there is something I have to ask you." Katie sat down on the bed and took a deep breath. "Brian wants me to go to a Grateful Dead concert on Saturday night. It's in Boston at the Arena. Oscar would drive us in and bring us home. *Please* can I go! Please, oh PLEASE!"

Mrs. Kelso gave her husband a worried glance. "Your dad and I will have to talk this over," she said. "There tend to be drugs and alcohol at concerts like this, Kate. Seventh grade seems a little young to go to a rock concert at the Arena alone at night."

"I wouldn't be alone. I'd be with Brian."

"Your mother and I will discuss it," said her father, tapping his right foot. "Rachel, do you feel up to going downstairs to eat supper?"

"Of course I can eat downstairs. Kate, be a lamb and go set the table. Your dad and I need a few minutes alone."

Katie set the kitchen table for five and hurried back upstairs to brush her hair. She wanted to look her best when Oscar dropped off the geranium and the chocolate cake. Putting a dab of blush onto her pale cheeks, Katie realized that all she'd had to eat all day was a bite of Corky's sandwich. She slumped onto her bed and pictured arriving at a rock concert in a black limo.

The chimes on the front doorbell jolted Katie back from her daydream. She tied a pink ribbon in her hair and hurried down the stairs. Sam stood behind the glass front door carrying a large white box with both hands. Mozart's leash was clenched between his teeth.

"Wet me in," he mumbled without letting go of the leash. Katie opened the front door. Sam spit the leash out of his mouth and put the box on the hall table. He went back outside and handed Katie a geranium plant with five bright red blossoms.

"That box weighs a ton," he said, unclipping the leash from Mozart's collar. "Oscar said to give these to Mom. What's in it, anyway?" asked Sam.

"Open it up and you'll see," said Katie, carrying the geranium into the kitchen.

"Holy mackerel, look at this!" Sam lifted an enormous seven-layer chocolate cake out of the box. It said, "WELCOME HOME" in white icing on the top. All around the top, Emma had made red geranium blossoms out of icing.

"That's a piece of art," said Katie, staring at the cake.

"I'm glad it's not in a museum," said Sam, licking chocolate icing off his fingers.

For the first time in history, Mrs. Kelso allowed the children to drink soda instead of milk at dinner. Sam had a tall glass of Coke with no ice. Katie poured herself a diet soda so she could eat as much pizza and cake as she wanted. Willy knocked his ginger ale on the floor, and Mozart licked up the spill.

"This *is* a celebration!" Mrs. Kelso reached for her husband's hand. "Ironically, I've never felt happier, or had a better meal." Katie saw tears well up in her mother's eyes.

Mr. Kelso kissed his wife's cheek. "If I'd known pizza was your favorite meal, honey, I could have saved a lot of money on gourmet restaurants."

Katie stood up from the table and began to clear the dishes. She wondered why her mother felt so happy when she'd just had an operation for cancer.

"I'll do the dishes," said Katie as she folded the pizza box for recycling. Her dad lifted Willy onto his shoulders to carry him upstairs for his bath.

"Thank you all for everything," Mrs. Kelso said. Katie watched her mother stand up slowly and walk stiffly in her bathrobe to the stairs. "I am blessed to have the most wonderful family a woman could ask for."

After Katie finished her homework and wrote in her diary, she went into her parents' bedroom to say goodnight. Her mother lay under the covers, sound asleep. Her dad was reading a mystery book beside her.

"Did you decide about the rock concert?" Katie whispered.

Her father put down his book, climbed carefully out of bed, and tiptoed into the hallway.

"Your mother and I aren't very comfortable with this idea, Katie. Seventh grade seems awfully young to go into Boston alone on a Saturday night."

"I'll be careful, I promise, Dad."

"It's not that we don't trust you, Katie. It's just that there are so many unpredictable characters milling around at an event like this. Last week a boy was stabbed at a rock concert."

"But that was a heavy-metal concert, Dad. The Grateful Dead fans are peace loving. Deadheads take care of each other."

"What do Brian's parents think about all this?"

"Remember, Brian's parents are divorced. His dad lives in Hawaii and his mom is away on a business trip."

Mr. Kelso scratched his head. "I'm sorry, Katie. I'm afraid your mother and I feel we have to say no to this one. There will be plenty of other chances to go to rock concerts in the city when you are a little older."

Katie looked her father straight in the eyes. "Please, Dad," she said. "I know I can take care of myself."

Mr. Kelso tapped his right foot. "I'd prefer no further discussion about this issue, Kate."

"Night, Dad," Katie said coldly. She walked quickly down the hall and slammed the bedroom door behind her. Katie picked up her diary and added a P.S. to the page for September 21.

Dad makes me sooooooo mad! He says I can't go with Brain to the Ded Consert. He thinks Boston is to dangorous for us to be alone. If I can take care of Sam and Willy, why can't I take care of myself? This wood be the first reel bate of my life. Even if Brain isn't all that cute he's smart and risponsible and reely sensative. I bet I'm his best freind and I've only nown him for a few weeks.

The End

CHAPTER

22

Katie, Meghan, and Ping were the first students to arrive in homeroom on Tuesday morning. Katie unclipped the list of sixty vocabulary review words from her notebook and walked over to Ping's desk.

"You want me to drill you, Ping?" she asked.

"How about I drill you?" said Ping with a shy smile. "Mother and father drill me many hours."

"Sure," said Katie handing Ping her review sheet. "I put a star next to all the stumper words."

"Stumper. Why mean stumper?"

"Stumper just means the words I don't know, like they stump me."

"Like a tree?" asked Ping.

"Never mind," said Katie. "Just ask me the words." Katie smelled Spud's lemon cologne. She turned around and watched Spud take his seat in the back row. He was wearing a Red Sox cap turned around backwards and a T-shirt with a picture of a Budweiser beer can on the front.

"Hey, dude. What's up?" he announced loudly to Meghan.

"So Katie and the Jap are at it again," he teased, looking over toward Ping's desk. "Wee Wee Dung probably knows more English than you do."

"I don't see you getting straight A's in English," replied Katie, flipping her hair over her shoulder. "By the way, what happened when Mr. Cherry-Berry marched you out of the cafeteria?"

"Not much," said Spud casually. "My mom had to come in and have a friendly chat with old Doc Ward. I've got ninth-period detention for the rest of the month."

"What about football practice?" asked Meghan. "Aren't you on the J.V. team?"

"Pop-Eye will just be late for practice, that's all. Coach says my body is in peak condition. The opposition cringes at the mere sight of me." Spud flexed his bulging biceps.

"They aren't the only people who cringe at the sight of you," said Katie, turning her back.

"What's up, sweetie pie? Do I sense a chill in the air?" Spud walked over next to Ping's desk and put his tan right arm around Katie's shoulder. He gave her a gentle squeeze. "Sorry I stood you up on Friday," he whispered in her ear. "I hope you didn't wait too long."

"Don't worry," Katie answered.

"So, when are we going to the stacks?"

"Never," said Katie firmly.

"But there is so much I can teach you, sweetie pie," said Spud, running his fingers down her back. Katie tensed her muscles and pulled away.

"Get lost," she said.

"How about the movies? Would sweetie pie rather go to the movies than the stacks?"

"I said, 'Get lost!'" Katie sat down next to Ping. Spud sauntered back to his seat.

Miss Dalton and Brian walked into the classroom together. Katie imagined that they were discussing the literary magazine. Brian was probably trying to convince Miss Dalton to accept her as part of the staff, even though she'd been rejected by every voting member.

Brian walked over and tapped Katie on the shoulder.

"How come you didn't call me last night? I waited until after eleven for you to call me back."

"I'm really sorry, Brian. It got so late. I was afraid I'd wake Miss Gumpert."

"Well, can you come on Saturday night?" Brian asked eagerly.

"You won't believe this, but my parents won't allow me to go alone to a rock concert. Not in the city. They think I'm too young."

"But you're thirteen. I've been going to concerts by myself since I was nine!"

"Yeah, but you don't have parents like mine. They worry about everything."

"I guess that's true," said Brian thoughtfully.

"Maybe another time," Katie suggested. "Maybe we could go downtown to the movies one night."

"Sure," said Brian. He looked disappointed. He put his sunglasses back on and sat down in his seat when Miss Dalton rang the brass bell on her desk. After saying the Pledge of Allegiance and taking attendance, Miss Dalton walked around in front of her desk.

"Dr. Ward and I were delighted to see so many seventh graders try out for the *Golden Plume* editorial board," she began. "I wish we could accept each one of you, but the staff has voted to keep the group small and manageable." Miss Dalton cleared her throat. "At this point, I would like to announce the five seventh-grade students who were chosen yesterday for a one-year position on the board."

Katie could feel her heart pound under her corduroy jumper. She glanced at Brian and then looked quickly down at the floor.

"This year's *Golden Plume* editorial staff includes the following seventh graders: Brian Straus, Bambi Talbot, Stephen Mathews, Susannah Davis, and Katie Kelso."

Katie felt her heart lurch in her chest. Her palms were sticky. Brian gave her a quick smile and flashed a V for victory sign with two fingers.

"Congratulations to you five," Miss Dalton continued. "Of course, we are happy to print submissions from any G.W. student in the *Plume*."

When the bell rang for first period, Brian waited for Katie in the corridor. "Congratulations," he said. "I never doubted for a minute you'd be chosen."

"I can hardly believe this," said Katie.

Spud brushed by Katie as he walked out the classroom door. "Katie's joined the eggheads," he taunted as he passed by.

"That kid is a real nincompoop," complained Brian. "He's got the brain of a worm."

"Spud just puts his energy into sports, not books. He's been a jock ever since he was a kid," said Katie. "He'd be nice enough if he'd stop putting people down."

"I've had an idea about Saturday night," Brian said as he and Katie began to walk toward the north stairwell. "Do you think your parents would allow you to go to the Dead concert if Oscar came, too?"

Katie looked surprised. "Does Oscar like the Grateful Dead?" she asked.

"Sure! His son plays the guitar in a rock band. We listen to the Dead on the CD player in the limo all the time."

"That might make it okay," said Katie. "After all, Oscar is a responsible adult. As soon as my dad gets home from work tonight, I'll ask my parents. I'll call and let you know, I promise."

As they walked into first period English, Katie noticed that there was a map pulled down over the blackboard.

"A pop quiz!" she moaned.

"Call me tonight," said Brian. He sat down confidently at his desk and took out a sharp pencil from his Lucite pencil case.

Katie's mind wandered as she tried to answer the quiz questions on the homework assignment. She propped her head on her elbow and watched a fly buzzing at the window. She wondered if she should tell her parents about

Oscar before or after dinner. Her dad's mood usually improved after he'd eaten.

That evening, after Sam had washed the dishes, Katie sat down at the kitchen table next to her mother. Mrs. Kelso was drinking decaffeinated coffee and looking through a stack of get-well cards. Mozart was curled up in his basket by the refrigerator. Katie sensed this was a perfect moment.

"Mom and Dad, could I talk to you for a second?"

"What is it, Katie?" Her dad looked up from his newspaper. "I thought the rock concert issue was settled."

"I've got exciting news! I got accepted onto the *Golden Plume* literary staff. Only five seventh graders were chosen."

"That's terrific, honey," said her father, putting down the paper. "We're so proud of how well you've adjusted to G.W., especially considering all you've had to cope with here at home."

Mrs. Kelso beamed at her daughter. "Shall we tell her now, Jack? I mean about the birthday present."

"Go ahead, tell her now. October 20 isn't that far away."

"Your father and I have decided to let you choose a pair of 14-karat-gold earrings for your birthday," her mother said proudly.

"Really?" Katie gasped. "You mean, I can get my ears pierced? I thought I had to wait until I was in the eighth grade!"

"You've shown us very responsible behavior both at school and in taking care of your brothers." Mr. Kelso gave his daughter a hug. "We feel you've earned a special reward."

"I'm afraid I'll have to ask you to baby-sit on a pretty regular basis, Kate, once I start my radiation treatments."

"Don't worry, Mom. I'll help you. Just don't make it at tutoring time, or on Wednesday afternoon, when I work with the lit club."

"You tell me the hours that are best for you and I'll plan my appointments accordingly."

Katie cleared her throat. "I've got something else to tell you."

"More good news, I hope," said her dad.

"I told Brian I couldn't go to the Grateful Dead concert," Katie began carefully, "but he came up with a great idea. He said Oscar loves the Dead. He wants to go to the concert with us. He'll even sit with us!"

"What do you think, Rachel?" Her dad put his paper on top of the dishwasher and began to pace up and down the kitchen floor.

"Tell us more about Oscar, Kate," said her mother.

"He's a real gentleman. He says 'jolly good' and he always shakes my hand. Brian says he's been like a dad to him. Brian even gets to eat dinner sometimes with Oscar and his wife. They've been working for Brian's mom for ages, ever since Brian was a little kid."

"And he'd be willing to go to the concert with you?"

"Willing! He's *dying* to go! The Dead is his favorite rock group. He even has a son at some university in England who plays the electric guitar."

"She would be chauffeured in and out of town, Jack. It's certainly safer than coping with public transportation."

Mr. Kelso smiled. "If Oscar is willing to go and you feel mature enough to handle the crowds, I'll give my permission. Actually, I wouldn't mind being chauffeured into town on Saturday night myself."

"*You* can't come!" Katie grinned at her dad. "I'll call Brian. He's getting the tickets from a shaver."

Her mother looked perplexed. "You mean a scalper?" she asked.

"Yeah, that's it, a scalper. He can get tickets to anything, even the World Series on one day's notice."

Katie put her mother's coffee cup in the sink. "Thanks, guys," she said. "Do you think I could possibly get my ears pierced before Saturday night?"

"Absolutely not!" said her mother, shaking her head. "Not until October 20, your fourteenth birthday."

Katie pretended to dance like a ballerina as she pirouetted into the living room. She picked up Willy and gave him a piggyback ride up the stairs. Once Willy was in the bathtub, Katie told him the next adventure of Darby the dump truck.

"Telephone, Kate!" Mrs. Kelso called up the stairs.

Katie lifted Willy out of the tub. "Follow me," she said, wrapping Willy in a towel. Katie grabbed the telephone in her parents' bedroom.

"Hello?"

"I'm so jealous!" Katie recognized Corky's voice. "I wish I'd tried out for the lit magazine. When Miss Shapin told us in homeroom that you'd been nominated for the executive board, I couldn't believe it."

"Here's something else you won't believe." Katie's voice was quivering. "Mom and Dad gave me permission to get my ears pierced on my birthday, *and* to go with Brian on Saturday night to the rock concert. Oscar's coming, too. He's a genuine Deadhead."

"I don't believe it! You're going out on a date?"

"I knew I'd go on a date by Thanksgiving, but this is like a miracle. It's still September!"

"I'll rent the Grateful Dead video," said Corky. "We can see what people are wearing to their concerts."

"Up! Up!" cried Willy. With her hands around his arms, Katie pulled her little brother's slippery body up onto the bed. "I've got to go," she said. "I'm about to study my vocabulary review words with Mom."

Katie said good-bye and hung up the telephone. She dressed Willy in his racing car pajamas and gently lowered her sweet-smelling brother into his crib. "Dad will read you a story," she said.

"Night-night, Tee-Tee," said Willy. Katie kissed her brother on the cheek and started to hum her favorite Dead tune, "China Cat Sunflower." How could she possibly wait until Saturday? Saturday would be the most important day of her life, and this was only Tuesday.

CHAPTER

23

Every night that week, Katie played the Dead at high volume while she did her homework. She borrowed tapes from Corky and Brian. By Friday, she could hum every tune, even if she couldn't remember the exact lyrics to each song. On Saturday morning, Katie painted "Raspberry Red" polish on her toenails. She washed her hair and set it in giant curlers so she would look as pretty as the girl in the shampoo commercial.

Corky came over to help her decide what to wear. They chose blue jeans with a white turtleneck and Mrs. Kelso's green-and-orange sash woven by Indians in Guatemala. Even Sam seemed excited about Katie's date. He asked his friends Aly and Sandy over for a sleep-over so they could see Oscar's limousine in person.

At 5:30, Katie rinsed her mouth with breath freshener for the third time and took the curlers out of her hair.

"I can't go," she shrieked from the bathroom. "I look awful! My curls came out all wrong."

"You look lovely, dear," called her mother from the bedroom. "Just put a little water on your comb."

Katie put her hairbrush under the faucet and ran the soaking brush through her hair. The red chestnut curls fell limply to her shoulders. Grabbing her mother's Shalimar, Katie sprayed herself from head to foot over all her clothes and on her drooping curls. The perfume smell made her cough and sneeze. Katie ran out of the bathroom gasping for breath.

"Are you all right, dear?" her mother asked. "You sound as if you are coming down with a ghastly cold."

"I'm fine," Katie sputtered. "I think I'm allergic to Shalimar."

"You're supposed to just spray a tiny bit of perfume behind your ears and on your wrists."

Sam walked by, holding his nose. "You stink!"

"Now I'll have to change my entire outfit!" Katie cried.

"You don't need to change, love. Why don't you just stand outside for a second and air out."

Katie raced down the stairs and into the backyard. She peeked around the house and saw the stretch limousine pull up to the front curb.

"They're here!" shrieked Sam, racing to the curb followed by his two friends and Willy.

"I look horrible," groaned Katie, running back inside the house.

"You look fine, Kate," her mother reassured her. "Come introduce your father and me to Brian and Oscar."

"I can't go!" cried Katie, looking in the hall mirror. "I don't look a thing like the Dead fans in the video. People will know immediately that I'm from the suburbs."

Mr. Kelso opened the front door.

"You look beautiful!" Brian exclaimed, staring past him at Katie.

Mr. Kelso shook Oscar's hand. "It's mighty nice of you to take these young people into the concert," he said. "Mrs. Kelso and I feel a lot happier knowing you're along."

"It's my pleasure," said Oscar, tipping his cap. "Brian and I have been Dead fans for quite awhile now."

"Show them your shirt," Brian said proudly. "I gave it to him for Christmas."

Oscar looked at Mr. and Mrs. Kelso and grinned. He opened his jacket to reveal a multicolored tie-dyed T-shirt. The shirt had a skull pierced by a lightning bolt, and the words "Steal your face right off your head" written underneath.

"It's *beautiful*!" said Katie. Her parents laughed. "I'm going to buy one just like that with my baby-sitting money."

"They always sell tie-dyes at Dead concerts," Brian said confidently.

"Mom and Dad, this is my friend Brian." Katie switched her weight from one foot to the other.

"We are so pleased to meet you, Brian," said Mrs. Kelso, holding out her hand. "Katie has really looked forward to this moment all week."

All my life, you mean, thought Katie to herself.

Brian smiled and shook hands. "I've heard a lot about you, Mrs. Kelso. I'm glad you are feeling better."

"It looks as if you may have more Dead fans than you anticipated," said Mr. Kelso, pointing to the car. Sam, Willy, Aly, and Sandy were sitting on the back seat frantically pushing buttons. The windows were going up and down and the TV was blasting an "I Love Lucy" rerun.

"Say good-bye to Brian and Katie," called Mr. Kelso to the boys. "It's time for them to leave."

"Be sure to stay close to Brian so you don't get lost in the crowd," Mrs. Kelso said anxiously. "Katie sometimes gets lost," she explained to Brian.

"Oh, Mom!" said Katie, looking embarrassed.

Oscar opened the passenger door. Brian stood back as Katie climbed in first. They both waved good-bye as Oscar pulled the limousine away from the curb. Katie opened the window and called to her parents, "Don't wait up!" She sat back on the enormous black leather seat and buckled her seat belt. She tried to relax. *I've got to remember every detail*, Katie thought to herself. *This will make excellent short-story material.*

The evening air blew gently through the open window as they passed through the streets of North Kent. Katie waved to the man at the gas station and to the crowd of teenagers hanging out in front of Burger King. She saw Spud kicking his Hackey Sack. As the limo passed by, he froze with his foot in midair and his mouth wide open. Bambi and Stephanie waved. Corky had promised Katie she'd be walking Muffin up and down Lincoln Avenue shortly after 6 p.m. As the limousine sped past, Katie leaned out the window and waved frantically.

"Have fun!" shrieked Corky from the sidewalk.

Brian moved closer to Katie on the leather seat. He took her hand and held it on his knee.

"What happened to your fingernail?" he asked, glancing at Katie's right pinkie.

"Oh, that's my lucky finger," said Katie, tossing her windblown hair over her shoulder. She gave Brian's hand a squeeze.

"You're a very special person, Katie," said Brian, almost in a whisper.

Katie squeezed his hand again. She took a deep breath. It didn't seem possible. There she was, sitting next to a boy in a black chauffeured limousine, speeding toward the city on a Saturday night. In her mind, she was already writing the first line in her diary.

Setp. 26

Deer Dairy,

This has been the best day of my life! I went on my first reel date and I'm not even 14 yet. There was a terrible trafic jam on the way to the concert but Osker new a secret root. We still got to the concert in time for me to buy a purple tie-die G. Ded T-shirt. We sat up front near the stage. The music was so loud it made my teeth vibrate. I wanted to hold my ears. The fans crushed around us waving their arms like crazy and smoking and shreeking and some kids were dansing on top of there seats. I was almost skared but Brain held my hand. Osker wore ear plugs.

On the way home Brain and I had an unbeleavable talk. He says he's never had a gril friend. He says he thinks about me evry minut and he can't consintrate in school. Only a few weeks ago I wanted to go out with Spud and be a P.K. Now I think Brain is so much more inteligent and sensative and matur. I also relize how skared I feel about Mom's cansir and how important it is to be in a family. So many feelings are stored up inside me. I think I'll write more poeitry to give them a voice. Now elem. sckool seems just for little kids. I know I can be sucksessful at G.W. even if I'm not a P.K. I mite be in love. I don't dare tell Corky because she'll ask me evry minit what love feels like. Brain says my eyes are lovlier than buterflies in Africa. He is very romantic with me even thow we've only been going out one nite. I hope he'll like my Mom and Dad. Sometimes I feel even richer than Brain and all I've got left after bying that shirt is $7.00.

The End

About the Author

Caroline Janover grew up with a learning difference in a small town in New Hampshire. Her second year in the second grade, she invented her own private phonetic language and began to write nightly in locked diaries about her friends and feelings. Now the mother of two creative, intelligent, dyslexic sons, Caroline weaves real-life  experiences into fiction as she writes about young people and their families. She is also the author of *Josh: A Boy with Dyslexia* (Burlington, VT: Waterfront Books, 1988).

Caroline graduated from Sarah Lawrence College and received Masters Degrees from Boston University and Fairleigh Dickinson University. She currently lives with her husband in Ridgewood, New Jersey, where she is a Learning Disabilities Teacher-Consultant in the public school system. A recipient of the Governor's Outstanding Teacher Award, Caroline frequently lectures to children and adults about the perceptual problems and creative strengths of the dyslexic learner.

MORE FREE SPIRIT BOOKS

A Gebra Named Al
by Wendy Isdell
Julie hates algebra until she follows an Imaginary Number to the Land of Mathematics where the Orders of Operation are places, and fruits shaped like Bohr models grow on Chemistrees. Ages 11 and up; $4.95; 128 pp.; s/c; 5 1/2" x 7 1/2"

Making the Most of Today: Daily Readings for Young People on Self-Awareness, Creativity, and Self-Esteem
by Pamela Espeland and Rosemary Wallner
Quotes from figures including Eeyore, Mariah Carey, and Dr. Martin Luther King, Jr. guide you through a year of positive thinking, problem-solving, and practical lifeskills. Ages 11 and up; $8.95; 392 pp.; s/c; 4" x 7"

School Power: Strategies for Succeeding in School
by Jeanne Shay Schumm, Ph.D. and Marguerite Radencich, Ph.D.
Covers getting organized, taking notes, studying smarter, writing better, following directions, handling homework, managing long-term assignments, and more. Ages 11 and up; $11.95; 132 pp.; illus.; B&W photos; s/c; 8 1/2" x 11"

The Survival Guide for Teenagers with LD* * (Learning Differences)
by Rhoda Cummings, Ed.D., and Gary Fisher, Ph.D.
Advice, information, and resources to help teenagers with LD succeed at school and prepare for the future. Ages 13 and up; **Book:** $11.95; 200 pp.; illus.; s/c; 6" x 9" • **Cassettes**: $19.95; 222 minutes on 2 cassettes • **Book with cassettes:** $28.90

Find these books in your favorite bookstore, or write or call:

Free Spirit Publishing Inc.
400 First Avenue North, Suite 616
Minneapolis, MN 55401-1730
Toll-free (800) 735-7323, Local (612) 338-2068,
Fax (612) 337-5050
E-mail help4kids@freespirit.com